Listen, the Wind

Roger Mais

Edited and with an introduction by Kenneth
Ramchand, Professor of West Indian Literature,
University of the West Indies

Longman

Longman Caribbean Limited
Trinidad and Jamaica

Longman Group UK Ltd
Longman House,
Burnt Mill, Harlow,
Essex CM20 2JE, England
and Associated Companies
throughout the World

First published in 1986
Second impression 1988

ISBN 0-582-78551-0

Produced by Longman Group (FE) Ltd
Printed in Hong Kong

To *Jessie*, to *Karina Williamson* early friend of Mais's work and in memory of *Denis Sloly*

Contents

Introduction

Roger Mais (b. 11 August 1905, d. 1955)

ROGER MAIS was the fourth of eight children born to E.C. Mais
and his school-teacher wife Ann Louise (née Swaby). E.C. Mais
was druggist, businessman and farmer, and it was in this last
capacity that he took his family to live on an old coffee plantation
in the Blue Mountains when Roger was about seven years old. The
family returned to Kingston some time in 1918 but the years in
St Thomas parish were 'some of the happiest, as well as the most
interesting and adventurous years of my life.'

The years spent on Island Head plantation and on the smaller
estate called New Monklands in the same parish were formative
ones. There was early and dramatic knowledge of death. The oldest
brother went to Kingston and enlisted in the first contingent to leave
Jamaica for World War I:

> He never came back. The day the telegram came bringing
> news of his death, the world stood still on its axis. . . . The
> notion of death had been very remote to us. We could
> scarcely conceive of it reaching out a hand and taking Jim
> who would always venture more and was the strongest and
> tallest. . . .

But there was also the rhythm of life on the farm.

The young addict of *Blackie's Science Reader* spent many quiet hours
avoiding farm chores and observing plants, trees, animals, birds
and insects. He swam with the other children in the river that ran
through the plantation, and went out at night after crayfish with
split bambo torches. Roaming the countryside on his own, or in
company, the young artist registered the changing faces of sky and

bush, absorbing influences from nature and natural processes, and forming impressions that shape or colour all his writings including those with an insistent urban setting. Sometimes, as in the story entitled 'City Stricken to the Bone', Mais emphasises the contrast between nature's endless renewal, and man's stale repetitions:

> The sun comes up over the hills, and morning lets her bare feet down upon the dew-wet, silvery broad swathes of Seymour grass where the wild blue pea opens with the vining morning glory on the stark rock spurs.
>
> The sun comes up over the city by the sea, and the warmed-over cadavers uncoil from sleep and the anodyne of uninhibited sex and give themselves over to the frustration and hunger and disillusionment and emptiness and panic and despoliation and decrepitude and deception of another day.

One of the products of Mais's exposure to the natural world was a reconciling sense of pattern and process in spite of conflict and contradiction; and a major impulse in all his work is an attempt to give expression to contraries even while seeking to raise a consciousness of the underlying or essential harmony.

Anna Mais was not content to let nature be the sole teacher of her children. She conducted classes herself for the younger children; then, with the move to New Monklands they could attend the Trinity Ville Government Elementary School four miles away. Eventually the children were sent to boarding school in Kingston, and when the family moved back to the city, the fourteen-year-old Roger took up a place at Calabar High School where, three years later, he obtained the much-coveted Senior Certificate:

> I didn't make much use of my School Certificate. I never stayed long in a job. As in school, I hated the discipline, the people, the futility, the waste, the stupidity. Most of all, the stupidity. I went into the Government Service. I think if I had stayed there long it would have driven me crazy.

There were always vigorous and distinctive personalities in the large Mais family. One aunt 'waged an unremitting war with the flesh and the devil', and loved to sit in water with her clothes on. Another aunt had so many complaints it seemed that 'nature had just thrown her together somehow with a lot of old parts from some junk pile or other'; still, she was committed to carrying the cross represented by her husband to the end of her days, and kept the timid creature continuously reminded of it. The paternal grandfather learnt to play the harmonica in his eighties, instituted community singing on the front steps, and was struck by lightning at the age of eighty-seven when, armed with a hatchet, he climbed a mango tree to cut off a dead limb that offended his sight. The father represented authority, Victorian, immutable; but he was fallible enough to cultivate the image of his infallibility in the eyes of his children, aided by a wife who contented herself with quiet and tactful ironies.

Roger Mais was a character himself and began expressing his individuality early. After obtaining his School Certificate, he moved, apparently aimlessly, from one unlikely job to another. (A light fictionalisation of this moodiness and its radical causes can be seen in the story 'Look Where You're Going'). But a direction began to be indicated when he became a reporter with the leading Jamaica newspaper, *The Daily Gleaner*. It was inevitable that someone with Mais's strong moral outlook, and with his sense of the mystery and possibility of human life, should be an enemy of oppression, and just as inevitable that such individuality as his could not be counted upon to abide with tabulated creed, doctrine or manifesto. But it is clear from his short stories and articles in *Public Opinion* between 1940 and 1945 that he was a radical thinker committed to a remaking of Jamaican society, a commitment which included for a start an improving of the lot of the proletarian mass in the city and on its perimeters. *Public Opinion* was the organ of Norman Manley's People's National Party, and Mais's association with the journal and the people producing it placed him in the vanguard of the nationalist movement.

In 1944, Roger Mais became a national hero. With Jamaican forces fighting in World War II (as they had done faithfully in World War I, when Mais's eldest brother died), the Colonial Office issued its new constitution for Jamaica. To Mais, a nasty truth had at last become blatant – Churchill's declarations elsewhere were now translated into official policy: 'Time and time again,' Mais observed of Churchill, 'he has avowed in open parliament that . . . what we are fighting for is that England might retain her exclusive prerogative to the conquest and enslavement of other nations.' For, it was plain to Mais that what was being aimed at under the guise of making the world safe for democracy was 'the non-dissolution of a colonial system which permits the shameless exploitation of those colonies across the seas of an Empire upon which the sun never sets'. The article 'Now We Know' (*Public Opinion*, 14 July 1944) brought Roger Mais six months in St Catherine prison for seditious libel. Mais had only uttered with passion, eloquence, and courage what the majority of Jamaicans were feeling. The article was stencilled by the thousand and circulated throughout the island. Two collections of writings, *Face and Other Stories*, and *And Most of All Man*, published earlier at the author's expense, were suddenly in demand.

On his release from prison, Mais went quiet for a time – turning to painting and horticulture, and practising only a small amount of journalism. The exercise books for 1947 – 50 in the Mais manuscript collection, UWI Library, Jamaica – show that between 1945 and 1949 he was busy, reworking from a contemporary perspective, and in the form of plays, two kinds of material: that drawn from the classics which formed part of a Calabar High School education; and themes from the Bible which were part of his upbringing in a society nurtured on the Christian Book and in the home at the hands of parents who were members of the Non-comformist Fundamentalist Brethren Movement. By 1950, Mais had completed *Blood on the Moon* and *Storm Warning*, the first two parts of a projected trilogy which he intended to be about Kingston, Jamaica, and in which the characters and background would make up a picture that was 'three-dimensional, life-size, real'. The third part became *The Hills Were Joyful Together*, and when it was first completed it ran to more than twice the length of the novel of the same title which was published by Jonathan Cape in 1953.

Mais's energy was remarkable, and his creativity sought outlets in poetry, plays, short stories, novels and painting. But already in 1952, frustration and anger had set in. In July 1952, he announced a forthcoming exhibition of his paintings (held in July-August, 1952 at the Junior Institute, Kingston), divulged that *The Hills Were Joyful Together* had been contracted for publication, and served notice that he was leaving for Europe. Mais's farewell piece 'Why I Love and Leave Jamaica', indicated the complacency of the middle-class into which he was born. The piece could have been written in the 1980s as a despairing comment on the state of the arts and sciences in any of the islands:

> There is in this country, alas, a moated-tower of mediocrity, close and unassailable, and it holds such sway, it has acquired such a body of mediocre opinion about it that it is useless to try to make a dent in its smugness, and its exclusiveness, and its indifference to anything that does not come entirely within its limited scope and compass and influence.

On Tuesday, 26 August 1952, Roger Mais boarded the *Reina del Pacifico* bound for London, the West Indian literary capital of the 1950s where Edgar Mittelholzer (Guyana), Sam Selvon (Trinidad) and George Lamming (Barbados) had already wended their separate ways to partake of the pleasures of exile. With him Mais had the completed manuscripts of *Brother Man* and *Black Lightning*, and time was running out.

There were sojourns in Barcelona and Paris before 'that fascist disease', cancer, became rampant. Mais returned to Jamaica in 1954 and died the following year. As a gesture, his publishers had rushed out for him to see before the end, an advance copy of *Black Lightning*, his novel about the creative process and about the artist's relation to his community.

The Short Stories
Roger Mais's short stories are not well known because many exist only in typescript form in the Mais collection, UWI Library, Jamaica; and because those that have been published are in books and magazines now rare, defunct, or out of print. Mais published two collections at his own expense in the early part of his career: there was *Face and Other Stories* containing seventeen stories and

fifteen poems, and then came *And Most of All Man*, a collection of sixteen stories. The books are undated, and an article in a now defunct magazine published in Jamaica in 1952 when Mais was still on the island says they were issued in 1939 and 1940.

The next most important source for Mais's published stories is the journal *Public Opinion* where Mais published at least twenty-five stories between 1940 and 1945. Other scattered sources include: *Bim* (Barbados), scripts of the B.B.C. *Caribbean Voices* programme especially between 1946 and 1955; the English magazine *Life and Letters* especially the April 1948 and November 1948 issues; and Edna Manley's *Focus*, especially the issues for 1943, 1948 and 1956.

The stories chosen for this collection, as the Contents page indicates, come from the main published sources. They have been put into groups and arranged in an order that permits certain features of Mais's contribution in this genre to be demonstrated.

Part I

The stories in Part I have a function in this gathering as being a series of preludes setting out key ideas, motifs and feelings in the author's short stories and in his fiction as a whole. They are unusual when considered as stories for they contain little or no dialogue, minimal social interaction, and not much of a story line. For all this, Mais is able to suggest the existence and pressures of a social order but there is an inevitable movement towards some kind of renewal. In 'Jungle' and 'The Tramp' a concentration upon the introspections of the protagonists is accompanied by a use of symbolic elements intended to suggest the possibility of renewal through and after death.

The protagonist in the first, a young man who had been 'launched in the comparative security and respectability of the Government Service' would appear to be modelled upon the young Roger Mais, and there is an unusual intimacy between the narrating voice and the spirit of the fictional young man, who wants 'to live', 'to be free', 'to create something beautiful' and to write a book about life ('what was good in it, and what was wrong. And what was beautiful and gay and what was ugly'). The fictional young man had learnt from when 'he was ever so young' to address God as 'Lord' and he is encouraged by God ('That's the stuff, son') in his wish to live with delight and to be as 'spontaneous as the green idea of growth'.

The young man, however is torn between the demand for security and the deeper urge to live. Mais works with the protagonist's energetic anger to write with sarcasm about a society which prevents people from achieving anything more than a complacent and unfeeling existence because it is set up to deny the emergence of individuals:

> The world must go on. It doesn't matter about individuals as individuals. So the world, that social structure known as the world, must see to it that its young men and young women are kept securely inside the pen. It just naturally turns the cold shoulder to all who rebel against this and talk about their individuality, for who the hell cares about any one man's individuality, or whether any one individual is free inside himself, inside his own heart or not.

The story is convenient for showing the tie between Mais's criticisms of society and its source, which is a passionate concern for the fulfilment of the individual life. The young man's assertiveness, his fervent pontificating to a cheering God, the encounter with the young woman towards the end, and Mais's relaxed attitude towards him as a character in a story, save the piece from heaviness, and allow us to take delight in a slightly eccentric and charming fictional personage.

'Jungle' evokes the sinister qualities of the tough zones of the city at night through which a thoughtful figure, who knows its dark corners and how to place its sights and sounds, makes his way home. There is a pronounced tendency towards metaphor and symbol in this short vignette, though Mais is not above some obvious tee-ing up at the start to make sure the effects do not miss. At the simple level, the city is a jungle but the story is not content to rest there. The paragraph beginning 'Better he thought' and ending '. . . firmament of stars', bristles with nominal groups dealing with death. Death is a recurrent theme in Mais's writing as the proper perspective from which to view life, and to give it meaning and purpose as a process.

From this point, 'Jungle' turns into a hymn about initiation into death, and Mais interprets death as release, as purification, and as the attainment of ultimate knowledge. In the story there are two kinds of death, the ignoble one suggested in the image of being 'dragged down by the mangy dogs', and a heroic one that comes out of an encounter with a worthy foe, the tiger with his 'two great green eyes set wide apart'.

Mais wants to go further, however. When we are refracted by this awful symmetry we at last see life as continuous beyond death, and we are liberated from thinking of death as a terminus. Instead it is a point of transit: 'To undo the knot. To release the pent-up dark stream of tremendous nothingness. Terror of the night translated to knowledge. Translated to triumph. To sudden release, that is the loosing of one hold to take everlasting hold upon another.'

But Mais does not delay us in these philosophical speculations, however important they may be to him, and to us. The writer of fiction returns to the fictional character who is thinking these thoughts. The carouser, indeed, takes some comfort from the thought that the leap of the great cat would be preferable to the pull of 'the foul and sulking dogs', but at the moment he wants neither. He keeps to the safe middle of the road 'with an almost comical precision'. His thoughts may be full of darkness and death, 'But his feet were taking him home'.

The next story, 'Tramp', begins with four choric paragraphs lamenting and cataloguing the disintegration that has fallen upon human existence. Man's soul can only express itself in his material surroundings and in human relationships, but everywhere the greater has become imprisoned in the lesser; human relationships with the Janes and Thomases around have become sterile. There is no heart, 'no mind, no real contact anywhere . . . no comprehension anywhere. And no cohesion.' Men and women have lost 'the meaning of life, the meaning of direction, of process'.

Mais is obviously reorchestrating motifs we have already seen in 'Look Where You're Going', and the rhythmic urgency of the voice may well carry us to the fifth paragraph where we meet a character not described but referred to as 'he', presumably the tramp of the title (at least one of the 'tramps', the other begin the

action, as in 'Tramp, tramp, tramp' with which the story begins).
The tramp is troubled by the consequences upon his life of the
condition lamented in the first four paragraphs. He is troubled by
his inability to love and interact, for 'he could give nothing of
himself, bestow nothing anywhere'. He is, therefore, cut off from
the process of living, a ripe fruit 'unable to fall away, to make the
necessary sacrifice, the separation, to make way for eternal fruition
and newness, renewing himself again and again'. The tramp realises
also that he is a man separated from his woman 'as though divided
by oceans and continents, living on different planes of consciousness'. He has become part of a negation and false gaiety: 'The world
busying itself with all the known antidotes to boredom. People
asking to be made happy. To find happiness here ready-made for
them. Or else finding it in non-resistance to inertia.'

Fortunately, this poor soul has begun to awake. He understands
now that all the partying is only escapism, for 'you didn't come
here to appropriate to yourself large helpings of happiness, but to
learn about process, and through pain, and to make death a splendid
thing, beautiful with giving, which is the whole purpose of life'.
Mais's positives can be inferred easily enough from the list of the
tramp's failings and lacks. But Mais attempts in the rest of the story
to dramatise an experience that the tramp undergoes. The dark
night of his soul is about to break.

Desperate to give of the love and joy in him that is ready to be
bestowed but unable to yield itself, the tramp wanders from place
to place 'taking the dust of the city and the heat and the glare of
the sun, and the irritation everywhere' and 'taking all directions',
right up to the last direction and destination of all:

And so he walked until he came to a time and a place. And
he stood still in the present letting go of everything. The
time and the place and the process of getting here. Loosing
the knot, the enigma, the paradox, the irritation, all
attitudes but at last the one, the utterly receptive.

And the light broke about his head, and he took it in his
hands and whirled and whirled it round until it formed itself
into a loop for him to stand in, nowhere and, out of time,

on an elevation that was like a hill. At the centre of all, of endlessness and nothing, he stood upon that elevation, within the circle of light.

He saw the first peep of the bud on the green twig, saw it taking light from the source the sun and weaving it into a pattern. Uttering out of the joy at the core of it, the centre of creation . . .

The whole movement has to be read. Mais's concrete description of the tramp's death and rebirth and the visualisation of the all-embracing act of creation of which the tramp and an awe-struck witness are a part, are done in a simple and strong semi-Biblical prose. The episode invites comparison with Wilson Harris's description in radically different language and style of a similar experience, Donne's witnessing of his own dissolution and of the original creating act towards the close of *Palace of the Peacock*.

The transfigured tramp discovers now that he is to be 'the instrument of song at the lips of that singer', that he has received a commission to form again and again 'its pattern of wholeness and beauty'. But the tramp must also accept that he is a tramp 'in the midst of houses and men and interminable streets that lead everywhere'. Mais's fable of the high calling of the artist, his responsibility to sing the song of life and to include the Janes and Thomases in it ends with the hard-headed return of the now inspired tramp back to the familiar city, with 'a healthy appetite and the longing for human contacts again'.

Part II

The stories in Part II have an urban or suburban setting. In each of them Mais uses the setting to create a social atmosphere appropriate to the theme of the story; in each case the action is externalised to a large extent, and the interest comes from the interacting of characters in various types of social encounter. (The difference between these stories and those in Part I doesn't need to be emphasised here.)

The order and routine of the great house is disturbed in 'The

Crooked Branch' when Mr Pepper's children begin to think like
their peers and see the social difference between themselves and
the adopted child, Caleb. Caleb begins to be affected by the others'
perception of him, and in the following incident Mais shows the
human capacity for being at cross-purposes and in double states
as even more operative when things like race and colour
considerations enter the air:

> One day it happened that Junie saw him sitting in the swing
> in the garden. Just sitting, not doing anything, and she
> came up to him, feeling somehow pained because of the way
> he looked so lonely and unhappy.
> 'Why are you sitting there?' she said.
> And when he got up immediately and walked away
> without saying anything, it hurt her all the more. She was
> sorry she had spoken to him. It was as though her very
> presence had scared him away. And she felt so hurt because
> of the deep hurt that she divined in him, that she wanted to
> cry herself.
> There were certain differences between himself and the
> other children that Caleb began to notice now for the first
> time. Such as the fact that his skin was somewhat darker
> than theirs, and his hair more curly. And these things began
> to take on a certain significance in his mind, albeit almost
> unconsciously.

Towards the end, Mais lets Junie and Caleb discover that they are
in love. Mais's wish to stop the story, and the appalled Mr Pepper's
need to hurry the monstrous and embarrassing Caleb off the scene,
are achieved simultaneously. Mr Pepper banishes Caleb to a distant
country town with stern injunctions, conscious that there are other
reasons in the obscured history of the house which make the match
unacceptable:

> What good would it do, he thought, to tell him the truth,
> that he and Junie were half-brother and half-sister. Better
> not, he decided; the boy would obey him implicitly, he
> knew. He would go away – never try to see her or

communicate with her again.

Perhaps it was even consideration for his feelings that made Mr Pepper determine to keep the secret.

What was the sense in hurting him more than he need be hurt. *Destroying once and for all for him what was perhaps the one wholly beautiful thing in life that he had ever known.* [My italics]

Mais's irony does not quite seal off the story. The final sentence (italicised) is a desperate attempt to jerk the story back to what might have been its originating lyrical impulse, almost a confession by Mais that he fears he has taken us too far into a social situation laden with implications to be resolved within the compass of a short story; and putting the sentence in the thoughts of the unlikely Mr Pepper only reminds us of this. The suggestion that in 'The Crooked Branch', Mais writes more like a novelist than as a writer of a short story may be worth discussion in class.

There is more concentration and control in 'The Little Cobbler'. The encounter takes place in an ambivalent zone where two socio-economic circles overlap. Big business in the form of the Electric Shoe Repair Shop with its neon lights, sales gimmicks and invisible ownership (Pinero, the Cuban) is about to capture the field from small business represented by Zaccy and his cobbler's shop which is already an anachronism on the High Street. But from another point of view, Pinero is an emigré, conscious of his status as an outsider, striving too hard to avoid giving offence, and banking against rejection by amassing capital. These two socio-economic factors give solidity to the characters. Mais's acute social observation traces the logic by which Zaccy repudiates at the climax all the friendly works of Pinero, and the equal inevitability with which Pinero slides back into accepting that he will always be 'an inter-loper, a vulgar outsider'. But this is a story of human contact made and then lost, not one that encourages us to pass judgment on either of the characters. Mais uses omniscient narration, and moves from one character to the other in order to open up an ironic perspective that makes the reader aware of the many conditioning influences that can prevent human beings from letting themselves love and trust one another. In a moment that corresponds to the epiphanic moment some practitioners of the short story consider essential to the form, Mais allows the sense of loss to be registered in a moment of illumination for Pinero:

> He wanted to run after that hopeless figure, to take him by the arm, to pull him back to a place of security, to talk to him, to reason with him, to tell him of things he himself had never guessed at before, but knew now, intuitively with a flash of inspiration. But he knew that he dared not, that he had no place there beside that derelict chip of humanity.

With 'Lunch Hour Rush', 'Blackout' and 'Black Magic' Mais is closer to the texture and colour of city life. The settings of the stories range from city centre at midday in a crowded restaurant, to a bus stop in the suburbs at night, to the leisurely world of the casual verandah, golf course and race track. The skilfully evoked hubbub in the restaurant is the impersonal and unknowing chorus to an unequal encounter between native exploiter and exploited that Mais manages to convey all the more forcefully by letting it express itself through Millie's thoughts and feelings, and in the callous practicality of the restaurant owner. In 'Blackout', the encounter between a Black Jamaican and an American woman is presented centre-stage as it were, with no supporting noises and with the characters voicing the issues to each other's faces. The Jamaican's sharp assertion of his equality as a man is not at all an expression of doubt, but rather an attack on what he sees to be the assumptions of a young woman whose social experience might indeed have conditioned her to see a Black as less than man. Mais allows his economically less well-off character to pick up the half-smoked cigarette of his departed adversary because he wishes to drive home the difference between economic inequality and human worth. Neither of these stories requires the kind of characterisation that Mais practised in 'The Little Cobbler', but it is worth noticing how swiftly he conveys the sense of individuals and crowd in 'Lunch Hour Rush', and the teasing way in which he inhabits the conscious-ness of the woman as the dark figure approaches in 'Blackout'.

The narrating of 'Black Magic' is an interesting variant from Mais's usual method. A newspaper report of the finding of a man's hanged body and a lady's handbag is followed by the lady's version of her encounter with a down-and-out jockey. With exemplary tact, and almost with humour, Mais allows Ruth Marchmant's words to reveal the unfeelingness and indifference of her circle, and at the same time, to intimate to the reader the mortal blow her disbelief and her betrayal of his trust in her has finally dealt the already struck down and humiliated jockey.

The last story, 'World's End', shows a radical shift in mode. The encounter between the old man and the city comes over as the perennial encounter between man (age and youth, for he is accompanied by his son) and an empty world. The death of the donkey sends the old man berserk, and he takes on the mission of trudging nameless streets and faceless houses in the stark city, to tell his tale of woe, and to numb himself further upon the unfeeling responses of those he meets. The reader is left to sort out the balance between pathos and heroism in the old man's performance, and Mais's descriptive touches are subtle enough to suggest the cycles of time behind the present scene:

> Outside on the piazza the boy stood listlessly, watching the dusk closing in on the street, and the people coming and going, and sometimes stopping to greet each other passing the good of the day. A dray drove furiously down the street and people gave way on either side, so that the yelling drayman, flourishing and cracking his whip, seemed like a character driving through the opposing ranks of an enemy horde. The stars came out one by one and filled the city. Inside the shop, the old man babbled on . . .'

Part III

In these stories, the main characters are women with the equivalent of the experience of marriage, and it is possible to consider them as contributions to what is now called feminist literature. The three stories are narrated in the third person, and in each case the point of view is substantially that of the woman, but there is significant and considerable variation. 'Some Women Take a Whipping' has omniscient narration of an objective type – the character is observed from the outside, and there is no attempt either to interpret her movements or enter into her thoughts and feelings. In 'Listen, the Wind', the story is told more from the perspective of the woman, the omniscient author telling us what she is thinking from time to time. In 'Gravel in Your Shoe' the narrative voice imitates the thought-speech of the main character creating a sense of the mind of a reflective woman, recognising the natural course her life wants to follow, and thinking how to cope with the obstacles in the way.

The simplest-looking of this group is 'Some Women Take a Whipping' in which Mais scrupulously observes the rising of Sadie Blum's grief and its eventual outpouring. The chatter of the community contrasts with the bereaved woman's numb silence in the first part of the story. The second section is more descriptive in character. Here, Sadie's continued silence, and the withholding of authorial gloss or speculation about her inner processes, has the effect of making Sadie's actions seem discontinuous, jerky and quite disconnected from their context – the other elements making up the scene. This deprives them of normal meaning.

The objectivity thus achieved (there is no evidence Mais has any theories about this but it doesn't matter) is endowed with suggestive potential and a suspenseful quality (we don't know, and we want to know) so that the descriptions have the pulling effect of narrative. The effectiveness of this can be seen in the last ten paragraphs of the story from the sentence that begins 'The girl got up from the bed presently . . .' through to the final sentence ending '. . . the fierce hard sobbing of the woman on the floor.'

Sadie's grief, reminiscent of Rema's in *The Hills Were Joyful Together*, is heightened by her memories of a sustaining relationship with a considerate and loving husband. Mais occasionally presents instances of women who are treated with love and respect by their men (though not usually in the present of the story), but the woman expected to serve and give and not to want is the more frequent figure. In 'Listen, the Wind', just such a woman is shown at a turning point in her relationship with a stereotypically irresponsible and charming man. Gossiping tongues would have her leave her man, but there are moments in her life with Joel that bring to her mind a more powerful force than gossip, 'the fixed and constant idea of *her* Joel that she kept locked away in the secret place of her heart . . . the revelation of him that looked up at her and made demands upon all her women's store of compassion and faith and understanding'.

Mais does without the story-telling voice of an omniscient explainer in this story, but once again the movement of the narrative and the progression of feeling are conveyed by alternative devices. At first, the character makes no distinction, resisting the human gossip as well as the words of the wind that told of the evil to come, though these were 'her own words, shaped in her own consciousness'. At the end, she seems to have come to the threshold of some kind of awareness of the self-deluding nature of her idealisation of Joel, a point at which she can dare to listen to her own word-thoughts about the man. As he slips easily off to deep slumber after a night out without her, insensitive to her mood or feeling, the banging of the shutter that Joel has been meaning to fix for so long bludgeons her once more, and the wind begins to speak again. This time she does not turn over or try not to listen. The words are heavy with portent. 'And all that night she lay awake and listened to the wind.'

The beleaguered female in 'Gravel in Your Shoe' is beleaguered by other women, and her struggle is seen not as a struggle against the male, but as a struggle against all those forces that deny her personhood and her privacy as an individual. But Mais begins at the beginning, the level of physical survival. The material burden of providing for herself, three children, and a man not always able to find employment may be the least of the troubles of Mais's washer-woman protagonist. In the first seventeen paragraphs, nevertheless, Mais describes her as a yard-dweller in difficult material circumstances, using the opportunity to establish her as a particular person (her pride in her work, her aversion to Miss Mattie, her obsession with cutting down the ackee tree, her home-spun philosophy – *'it's not the mountain you're climbing that wears you down, but the gravel in your shoe'* – and her think-talking to herself.

She owns to having her troubles, just as men have their troubles but thinks it would be fatal for them to take it out on one another:

> She was a woman. Which woman didn't have her troubles?
> Her woman's troubles. But she wasn't going to tribulate
> over them. Men too had their troubles. Men's troubles and
> problems. If they both set up against each other, tribulating
> over their troubles, fretting each other to weariness that was
> worse than death, where was the sense of living? Was that
> living?

Her acceptance of her role with respect to children and to her
husband comes not from reasoning about it or learning it
laboriously, but from a deep-down and trusted sense of its fitness
(if it feels right . . . ?), a sense which would also tell her without
reasoning or learning when it was not fit or acceptable. (To those
who are free, this a more flexible and forceful stance than any -ism
can supply.)

But ultimately Mais is concerned with the person, and his female
protagonist sees herself as a person committed to fullness of being:

> She would cut off her right hand – well, her right leg,
> anyway – to preserve above the reach of adversity, above the
> clutch of doubt or fear, above the threat of what might come
> that which to her was the burden as well as the song of
> being, of living. To preserve that whole, the whole thing in
> its entirety, that was what it meant to live. She had found
> out that herself. She had not learnt it laboriously, or
> stumbled upon it in the dark. She just knew it with the rest
> of knowledge about things, yourself, life, that is yours from
> the beginning, timelessly. . . Nothing could shake, or destroy
> that out of her.

Mais does his best to give his character independent life, and 'Gravel
in Your Shoe' is a successful dramatisation, but it is palpable that
he is also using the character to articulate a philosophy very close
to what we can infer to be the author's philosophy. It is this
underlying philosophy which gives urgency and passion to Mais's
social protest, and it is this which also tells us that for him social
reform was only a beginning. One belongs to the group or
community, but there is an ultimate aloneness and privacy, a private

space necessary to the unique individual. 'She wanted to live among them like neighbours, with love. A woman had her troubles, her bread to eat in secret that no one might share. No one. Her life to live. The beginning and end of living, and all that lay between.'

Part IV

The stories in Part IV reflect a common trend in West Indian societies, the drift from country to city. The focus is on the situations of young adults who have made the long march from the country-side only to find things turning out differently from what their hopes had been:

> She hadn't known it was going to be like this in the city. Else she wouldn't have left home in the first place. Short of them hog-tying and dragging her here. She hadn't known her brother meant to lock her inside a house and not want her to see anyone from outside, and not want her to have any friends or go anywhere.

In 'Look Out' the narrative proceeds from the consciousness of a tense and frustrated young woman; 'Red Dirt Don't Wash' is done from the point of view of an innocent whose fascination with city polish and a powdered city woman comes to an end with an act of liberation and self-discovery: 'Back there he belonged, where there was red dirt, everywhere, and the people didn't go around wearing shoes. . . . It was clean, the red dirt of his land, the place of his birth.'

As the titles announce, both stories intend symbolic effects. In 'Look Out', the moon is associated with lunacy, and the brittle mental state of the young woman; in the second story the red dirt of the village is presented more insistently as that which is wholesome and authentic, and it is contrasted with the powder that the ravished Adrian watches Miranda dusting her body with.

Repetition is a major device in each story. Incremental repetition of a word, the word 'nothing', is used in 'Look Out', coming to a climax in the last sentence. In 'Red Dirt Don't Wash' the repetition occurs around a pair of yellow boots. The yellow boots

Adrian had given up when he was younger (a present from his grandfather) repeat in Adrian's courtship of Miranda, and is associated with his wish to be a city man and Miranda's lover. His liberation from both obsessions, and his rediscovery of his true self is enacted in the shredding of the new boots into thin strips: 'He looked down at the jagged strips of leather in his hand, and his face became wonderfully luminous. He even smiled.'

Part V

The stories in Part V have a rural setting. Mais does not allow us to forget the rigours and the uncertainties of existence in a rural economy, and he conveys the flavour of country life in a socially realistic way through description of people, places, things; through imagery drawn from nature and from domestic life; and even through the voices of his characters. But in these stories he is hardly concerned with social interaction, poverty, or any of the issues related to day-to-day commerce such as we find in the urban stories. There is an animism in the rural stories (see, as an emphasised instance, the story 'A Tree Falls') which is one of the signs that the drama in the rural stories is of a different kind. For in Mais's rural world, the encounters are encounters between man and large forces outside of man, as well as powerful and mysterious ones inside himself. We can summarise the effect of this upon characterisation by saying that in the rural stories Mais is less interested in defining the characters as social entities than in exploring and expressing states of consciousness. For all this, Mais's rural world is solidly evoked.

Its mental and physical boundaries are plotted out, conveniently in 'The Ranger', an extended narrative of a basic type whose appeal lies in a graphic ballad-like sequence of events, and in the events themselves which belong as easily (and disconcertingly) to the natural as to the supernatural sphere. The tale of the arrival and occult influence of a stranger among a banana plantation community, and of his removal by powers applied to *in extremis*, is imbedded in a realistically portrayed rural environment not much different from a typical agricultural arrangement of people and commodities. The shady dealings of the newly appointed ranger,

Thomas, the sense of an underlying sexual tension between Mabel and the stranger, and the antagonism of Thomas towards Ephraim, who is Mabel's husband as well as an economic rival, are carefully set down by Mais to provide a realistic rationale for the figure that is Thomas, his abnormal doings and his uncanny end.

The generalised portrayed of agricultural life serves its function as atmosphere and context without drawing much attention on its own account. Not so in 'The Miracle' where it is the source of the stasis with which the story begins. Having failed in his attempt to combine agricultural work with a trucking business, and now convinced that the young wife he has married will not bear him a child at this late stage in his life, Henry subsides into a dull acceptance of a prospectless existence as peasant or slave (whose description shows us that Mais was never in danger of idealising rural life):

> His was an animal acceptance of things . . . his the routine of the beast of burden. He worked hard all day knowing that it earned him a square meal and a full night's rest. Each day brought its own fulfilment at the end. There was nothing outside of that . . . no promise outside of that, that an aggregate of many days of uninspired, uninterrupted toil might fulfil.

His wife Sarah goes along with this dogged life, but she has not let go:

> She went about this (her tasks) with mechanical lifeless motions that lacked enthusiasm, and yet she sang in a pure clear contralto as though giving expression to something deep within her that held all her store of hope, and courage, and inspiration . . . something beyond the dull mechanics of existence, that kept her spirit aware, and the flicker of hope alive and vivid against the medium-grey of her immediate and material outlook.

Thus Mais sets the stage, not for a story of economic revival, but for a radical encounter between loss of vision on the one hand, and faith in life's possibilities on the other.

In Mais's rural stories, an innocent description of tree, plant, hill or sky can unexpectedly take on a symbolic character. Henry and Sarah finish another day's work and set out for their house. 'They had a long way to go over a narrow and stony track.' Sarah's attempt to restore her husband to life is full of risk, and Henry will need to digest bitter roots:

> For this thing that she had deliberately brought upon herself, she had done out of the wholeness, the wonder, and the immaculation of her love for him . . . to awaken within him a new courage, a new confidence . . . to give him life again, and hope again. And in very truth it was a miracle. It was a sacred miracle of miracles . . . it was the miracle of immaculate conception.

Neither Henry nor the reader is likely to believe in immaculate conception. When told of the conception, Henry walks silently out into the night. When he returns, he embraces his wife in acceptance, fear and gratitude. Mais's prose soars above the known and the unknown facts in the case to celebrate Henry's acceptance as a humbling access to grace and vision: 'It was a revelation that came and went like the opening and shutting of a blade of lightning in the sky of night. Almost before he was aware of it, it was gone. And yet it seemed to open up now potentialities of understanding with his mind', and he longs 'to stand bathed completely in that light again, to feel the comfort and warmth and poignancy of it, and the sustaining wholeness and presence of it.'

A river in flood sustains another elemental battle in 'Flood Water'. The dependence of the farming community upon the river, and their vulnerability to its vagaries make them liken it to a woman. Boy Peters has swum across the river in flood once before, and the old man' Lijah warns him of the danger of taking it for granted he will do so successfully again. The terms make the river sound like life itself: 'Once you win, not to say you win all the time. Some day she goin' to pull you under.'

But Boy Peters has been infected by the suggestion that his wife is being unfaithful, and he is determined to cross the river and go to her. As he plunges into the currents, the innuendoes assail him:

'The roar of the rapids. The thunder of death in his ears. He would be broken to ribbons on the rapids. The rocks. His skull smashed in. His limbs all but torn from his body.' Boy Peters's determination to cross the river, then, becomes the mortal battle against doubt and distrust, the struggle with the river symbolising the struggle with primitive feelings unleashed in himself. These symbolic figurings do not prevent Mais from writing in concrete terms and realising the swim and the emotions vividly.

When the turmoil ends, Boy Peters is humble about his survival ('He would never boast about being able to best the old river, never again'), and exultant that he is alive. In this spirit he turns to go 'up the narrow pass – to home, the warmth of a fire, and the woman he loved, preferring death to the thought that he might share her with another'.

In 'A Tree Falls' Mais abandons metaphor and symbol and begins the story with the present tense, the 'is' preparing us for the literal presentation of the life or spirit of the forest which a lumberman trespasses against, a mortal sin which brings an implacable judgment down upon him. The progress of the axe against the giant mahogany tree is punctuated by a series of sounds and movements dismissed and ignored by swelling pride and presumption:

> The great tree trunk that had mocked the strength of his
> arm, and the silence that had mocked his puny laughter
> . . . they belonged to the stubborn reluctance of the
> unyielding wilderness, his ancient antagonist. But he would
> show them who was conqueror here, wilderness or man . . .
> heart of tree, or blade of axe . . . He would show them . . .
> *show* them . . . *show* them . . . !

Mais writes so convincingly of this encounter that like the sawyers who come at dusk and find the two bodies, we know this is no accident: 'They stood with bared heads and tight lips, staring at him. The silence . . . the snapping of dried twigs . . . the ghostly whisper of leaves all these daunted them . . . They left him where he lay within that vast, that weirdly peopled sepulchre of silence.'

The last story in this group seems to make elaborate play with the notion of a surprise ending. Three task-workers agree to a game arising from a thanksgiving sermon they have listened to. Each man must go home, observe some particular blessing in his life to be thankful for, and return to tell about it the next day. Jeremiah tells his blessing with relish, and Lucas, inspired by envy offers 'a wonderful tale'. Jake tells a dream which contains the answer to what he should be thankful for, and the answer is that it 'hasn't happened yet'.

Mais lays down sufficient evidence that Jake is not an ordinary task-worker in the first paragraph, and at the start of his narration we are told that it looked as if 'he was not looking at them so much as through them, and beyond them – way up the road and beyond the last end of it, and beyond the ends of all the roads with which it was joined, or by which it was intersected'. All this is indicative enough on a second reading, as is the authorial statement that Jake tells his story 'without a trace of dialect'.

But in 'The Glory Road' Mais uses the rural setting, the tradition of talking, and lying, and telling dreams, to write what turns out to be, metaphysically, a story about a man's meeting his death without fear, as the blessing for which he ought to be thankful.

Part VI

The relationship between men and women is a recurrent feature in all literatures. In Mais's work the two main emphases may be seen in the presentation. In the first place, Mais tries to give expression to the complexity of a relationship which contains powerful instinctual urges, romantic yearnings having to do with a deep-rooted longing for fulfilment in a better life, and strong social and rational motives arising from a conscious consideration of the kind of life we want to live in a given social context. These elements are often shown in conflict with one another, with the characters in varying degrees of confusion. A second emphasis which does not exclude the first comes from the writer's persuasion that in a tragic world, the love between man and woman has value as a sustaining force, and can help the individuals in their pursuit of fulfilment.

The last group of stories in this collection concentrate on the relationship between male and female. In the three stories, the author uses third person narration, sometimes omniscient, and sometimes limited to the point of view of the character. This does not mean that the stories are straightforward or lacking in subtlety. In 'For Ever and Ever', the author deliberately leaves the relationship between Etta and Mr Hurd out of the reader's sight, and at the climax he does not explain Etta's state or analyse her motives, so that we only know what Joe sees and hears, not even what he thinks. Now that she is pregnant, Etta is willing to marry Joe. The young man is ready, but 'somehow the realization of his life's happiness coming so suddenly and unexpectedly this way, brought no upsurging relevation of joy with it. Not as he would have expected it to. Perhaps it was because it had all happened so suddenly. He hadn't time to prepare for it. That was it. That was all.' In the last five sentences, Mais is narrating from Joe's point of view and reporting his process of thought, a procedure which allows us to notice an attempt to rationalise away a misgiving of some sort. When Etta follows up, and makes Joe say that he will love her for ever and ever, no matter what happens, the author allows the character to repeat the catechism, without direct comment, but with the seemingly descriptive phrase 'with anguish in his voice'. All of this, added to the fact that the story is entitled 'For Ever and Ever', makes the reader wonder: is Joe simply terrified at what marriage can mean, or has the thought crossed his mind that he is not the father of the child who has been conceived?

Mais's ironic attitude here does not imply that love is not worth much, only that the relationship can be full of uncertainties and ambiguities. The power of love, it should be noted, makes Joe suppress whatever doubt has entered his mind. In 'Just a Little Love, a Little Kiss', Mais uses omniscient narration again, this time to give lyrical expression to the longing for love or fulfilment. The story ends bitterly – the man shoots a dog and is reported to the police by the woman. He goes away, and she remains without hope, without comfort. But when the teacher first arrives to live in the house adjoining hers, and when she realises that the teacher is drawn to her, the thirty-seven year old spinster is joyful. She plays and sings to his profile one night: 'But it wasn't so much the words or the music as herself revealed to him. Herself flowing out toward him in the wonder and beauty of longing and fulfilment; in all the mystery and meaning of a dream.' The teacher, too, has his peaking as he stands on his side of the fence, 'a man made restless and haunted with unconscious emotions that moved him with unfulfilled longings, and all the restless years of vagrant desires and idle dreams'. Love is rejected by the teacher (because of the trauma the change would bring?) and the spinster is unrequited and finished (pehaps it was all an illusion), but the two moments remain as the centre of the story and as an expression of love's transforming potential.

In the third story, the omniscient narrator, except for one forgivable indiscreet paragraph, lays down all knowledge of the world in an engaging account of a young boy's discovery, after an older girl has gone away for good, that 'he loved her as he would never love another'. The narrative's description of the sweet pain of unattainable love is unwavering in its sympathy and belief:

> He grew thinner and more silent as the days went by. He knew, once and for all, that he would never be able to forget her. Not if he lived to be a hundred. And at the same time there seemed nothing in life left for him to live for. In the night it was worse. He would sit up in his bed with the cover drawn about his knees and stare out into the darkness and see only her face. Every moment and fleeting expression of it. Every incomparable, least, transitory shade of expression, of light and laughter, of mingled mischievousness and loveliness not to be told again.

None of these stories has the conventional happy ending, but they are effective as stories, and as concretisations of love's nature and love's possiblities.

Kenneth Ramchand

Bibliography

Writings by Roger Mais

And Most of All Man (short stories), Kingston, Jamaica, n.d.

Face and Other Stories (short stories and poems), Kingston, Jamaica, n.d.

Short stories from *Public Opinion* 1940–45, xerographic copies in West Indian Collection, UWI Library, St Augustine, Trinidad.

The Hills Were Joyful Together, London: Jonathan Cape, 1953.

Brother Man, London: Jonathan Cape, 1954.

Black Lightning, London: Jonathan Cape, 1955

The Three Novels of Roger Mais, London: Cape in association with Sangsters, Jamaica, 1966.

Relevant non-fiction

'Now We Know' in *Public Opinion*

'Why I Love and Leave Jamaica' in *Public Opinion*

Writings about Roger Mais

Hearne, John, 'Roger Mais: A Personal Memoir' *Bim* 6 (1955), pp. 146–50.

Lamming, George, 'Tribute to a Tragic Jamaican' in Wilmot, Fred.

Spotlight Magazine, 'Jack of all Trades', Jamaica, 13 (1952), pp.21–3.

Kyk-Over-Al

Public Opinion

Brathwaite, Edward, Introduction to Roger Mais, *Brother Man*, Heinemann, 1974.

Braithwaite, Edward, 'Jazz and the West Indian Novel', Part III, *Bim* 12 (1968), pp. 115–26.

Carr, Bill, 'The Novels of Roger Mais', *Public Opinion* (Jamaica), *Roger Mais Supplement*, 10 June 1966. 'Roger Mais – Design from a Legend', *Caribbean Quarterly* 13 (1967), pp. 3–28.

Creary, Jean, 'A Prophet Armed' *The Islands in Between*, ed. L. James, OUP, 1968, pp. 50 – 63.

D'Costa, Jean, *Roger Mais*, Longman, 1978.

D'Costa, Jean, Introduction to Roger Mais, *Black Lightning*, Heinemann, 1983.

Grandisen, Winnifred B., 'The Prose Style of Roger Mais', *Jamaica Journal*, (1974), pp. 48–54.

Lacovia, R.M., 'Roger Mais: An Approach to Suffering and Freedom', *Black Images* I, pp.7–11. 'Roger Mais and the Problem of Freedom', *Black Academy Review*, Fall 1970, pp.45–54.

Lewis, Rupert, 'Roger Mais Work as Social Protest and Comment', *Public Opinion* (Jamaica), 6 March 1967.

Moore, Gerald, *The Chosen Tongue*, Longman, 1969, pp. 85–95.

Morris, Daphne, Introduction to Roger Mais, *The Hills Were Joyful Together*, Heinemann, 1981.

Ramchand, Kenneth, 'The Achivement of Roger Mais' in *The West Indian Novel and its Background*, Faber, 1970 pp. 179–88.

Ramchand, Kenneth, 'The Hills Were Joyful Together', *An Introduction for the Study of West Indian Literature*, Nelson, 1976 pp. 13–26.

Williamson, Karina, 'Roger Mais: West Indian Novelist', *Journal of Commonwealth Literature* 2 (1966), pp. 138–47.

Part I

Look Where You're Going

HE walked down the street slowly. His hands in his pockets. A very serious young man. It takes a lot of courage to face the future without security of any sort. And sometimes his courage failed him. At such times he forgot that life was a gay and glorious adventure. And all a man needed to do was to live clean, and be free in his own heart.

But you can't be free, with security. Not really free. Because security implies responsibility. And responsibility perplexity and the continuous and progressive acquisition of the world's goods, and more perplexities again.

But just the same it takes a lot of stern courage to face the world and the future utterly without security. It made this young man stop living sometimes and start thinking about a lot of things, when he should have been thinking about something else.

What he should have been doing was walking with a swagger, a song on his lips, as the saying is. Even if he could do no better than barely turn a tune, whistling. He felt, for no particular reason, guilty. He felt, now what he really needed was a job. Something steady. And still, deeper down he knew this was all wrong, of course. And he longed to be restored to his freedom, and his innocence again.

Therefore he was unhappy.

It was night. A few stars looked down. There were a few people walking about, but only a few. There was laughter from a little house dimly lit somewhere over on the right. A woman laughing. Life was going on around him just the same. Untroubled, uninterrupted. But nothing pleased him tonight.

In the shadow of a kindly tree that grew inside somebody's garden he could see the dim outlines of a man and a girl. And there was no cop around. Nothing to bother them. Just a couple of no 'counts with no place to go.

Little things like that were usually the things that moved him deepest. They disturbed him, but delightfully. They made him feel that life was all right. But tonight it was different. And this difference was all a part of this new calculativeness. This awareness of un-innocence. He was like a wild animal irking at its freedom, longing to be back inside the pen.

He had started out life on his own bottom, as the saying goes, voyaging in safe waters enough. He had been launched in the comparative security and respectability of the Government Service. But in less than no time, as such things go, he was out of a job.

He had known from the very first that he could never fit in comfortably in this life of easy security. It was not for him somehow. He had quit the job suddenly and gone home feeling remarkably gay and full of beans, as they say. As though he had just done something really big. He knew that he would never go back there again. For one thing they wouldn't have him.

Since then he had tried about a hundred other jobs. Or maybe it was a million. But always one thing or another went wrong.

And then one day he thought, the hell with jobs. I don't want a job. I want to live. I want to create something beautiful, if it be nothing more than the words of a song in a girl's heart. A song about love. He was in love.

But it didn't last for long. For with it came the demand for security. He tried again, of course. He got another job. And he stayed in it and saved some money. He even made a down payment on a half-acre lot in a more or less fashionable suburb. And every day he grew sadder and sadder. And naturally the girl too grew sadder and sadder. For they were very much in love.

Until one day he decided, the hell with marriage. I want to be free. I want to live my own life. And love a bit, and laugh a bit. And take the hard knocks with the rest. And keep my innocence and my courage, whole. The hell with all this security, he said, I'm outside the pen, this time for good and all. She had just handed him back his ring.

He decided he'd write a book.

Now there was something he'd always wanted to do, he said.

He planned how he'd set down all the things he'd learnt about life, in the book he was going to write. What was good in it, and what was wrong. And what was beautiful and gay, and what was ugly. He'd leave nothing out. Nothing would be too insignificant to find a place in his book. It might be a best-seller, and he'd be made. He didn't care much one way or another. He knew of course that having money meant security, and the end of freedom. And the taking up of responsibilities, and the knowledge of guilt upon his conscience for having sold his wonderful freedom for some chips, and the loss of much of what is spontaneous in life, and innocent.

But he'd write his book just the same. The hell, he said, I could always give away the money. And I would still have my freedom and my life, and my innocence and laughter, as a young man.

He wanted to create something beautiful, most of all. Perhaps he didn't have as much religion as he might have had, for a young man in his circumstances, inside the pen. But he was by no means an infidel. That is to say he knew about God because he had acquired the habit of talking to him. He knew him personally, not as some awful deity; and perhaps a little familiarly, as a friend, an equal. In his wildest moments, when he became fervent to the point of hilarity, he would talk to him something like this:

Lord, he would say, I want to be one of the debonair whose inheritance is the earth, as they say. I want to do the maddest, gladdest things, just for the fun of it. To take the delight of it straight to others, just as light carries its luminance to all the objects that come within its radius. And never to do a mean thing. To fear nothing so much as the naughty slip into some little meanness, that is more often than not sheer stupidity.

And God would answer him right back, that's the stuff, son.

Lord, he would say. For he always called him 'Lord' at the beginning of a speech. It was one of the things he had learnt from he was ever so young, and he'd never been able to drop it. Sometimes he would say 'Father', only that sounded a trifle formal. But he figured 'Lord' was all right. Why, there were chaps not good enough to wipe your boots, who were called 'Lord'. It was a handle, it didn't matter.

Lord, he would say, I want to be just the gayest, maddest, person in the world. I want it as much as the next fellow. To be spontaneous as the green idea of growth. And to know goodness as the tree is glad of the burden of its bearing. Knowing that at last there are no exclusive persons, and no such thing as special privileges for anyone. Neither here nor hereafter. Seeing the gladness and goodness heavy on all the branches all around. And on every single branch and twig in the whole green universe. And the wind carelessly lifting the branches and tossing them, one toward the other, in the bravest, gayest of salutes.

Maybe you think this sounds a brash manner of speaking for a young man of no account to be addressing God. But he didn't think so. And that's what matters in the last analysis.

The book didn't get written all at once. Every once in a while he would become a backslider. He'd go back inside the pen again. And each time he came out, he'd swear it was the last time.

But it takes a mighty lot of courage to face the future without security of any sort. There is order too, and a definite plan in all this. Otherwise the world would soon become full of young men and young women of no account. And this wouldn't be good for society.

And society must go on. The world must go on. It doesn't matter about individuals, as individuals. So the world, that social structure known as the world, must see to it that its young men and young women are kept securely inside the pen. It just naturally turns the cold shoulder to all who rebel against this and talk about their individuality, for who the hell cares about any one man's individuality, or whether any one individual is free inside himself, inside his own heart, or not.

That's not what society is for, the young man said to himself, as he walked along slowly, not going anywhere. He was feeling very dejected with the loss of his courage with the fear of hunger and the sulking future that lurked somewhere ahead of him. All the way down the road.

He was looking down at his boots, so he didn't see where he was going, until he bumped right up against someone.

'Why don't you look where you're going?' It was a young woman, and she spoke with irritation.

He thought, well if she had been doing such a hell of a lot of looking it ought to have been enough to serve for both of us. But he only said, 'I am sorry'.

'It's okay,' she said.

Then she laughed, and went on.

He walked about three paces and then turned his head to look at her. And caught her in the act of just looking the other way.

He wanted to turn back then and walk along with her. Perhaps she was just as lonely as he. Perhaps she too was feeling depressed about the future. And afraid.

Perhaps each could lend the other a little hope, a little brightness to help him along the way.

The hell, he thought. They not only reject us, but they teach us the sort of manners that cause us to reject each other, even though we're on the same bit of timber drifting in the same wide open sea.

That's so's to make it tough for young men and young women to take their lives into their own hands, and their destinies, and live innocent, and free. If we could get together now we might even be able to start something on our own. A sort of rival society of divine vagabondage. And *they* are smart enough to know it.

Why don't you look where you're going? she had said. Well, why didn't *she*? The answer was simple enough. They were headed nowhere. They had no direction, nothing. No place to go.

The hell, he thought, why not turn around and catch up with her, and start talking to her, anyway.

But by now she was lost to sight around the first bend in the road. Beyond the place where the big tree grew inside somebody's garden, but cast a shadow large enough to suffice for a man and a girl in love with each other – just a couple of no 'counts, with no place to go.

Jungle

WALKING home at half-past three in the morning he heard a shriek, as of someone taken with terror, or pain. It might have been the cry of a wild animal. He had read somewhere that certain monkeys, when they fall prey to one of the big cats of the jungle, give voice to just such a scream. Almost human.

All round him the city slept. The figure of a man stretched out prone on the sidewalk in front of a Chinese shop made a dark blur. And the blurred whispers of sounds . . . sounds from the gully-course, the *riff-riff* of the wind going over the treetops and over the house-tops, the blurred jungle-sounds of prowling dogs about garbage.

And again the far away cry. Like an animal in pain, or in terror of death. The cry of a child, maybe, or of a woman. More likely a woman, he thought. It sounded eerie in this sleeping jungle of men, at three-thirty in the morning.

He walked with his hands in his pockets. Taking care to keep to the middle of the road. Between the tram-lines. He walked as though he was very tired. Stumbling a little. As though he had come a long way.

Three times in all he head the cry. Then it died down altogether and was lost. Died down like the wind that is lost in the vast empty stretches of night. Beyond the circumference of things; the stars, like branches in heaven hanging with fruit; lost beyond knowledge or count of man.

The night-jungle continued to issue its noises. Dogs scuffling among overturned garbage cans and boxes in bleak-looking tenement yards. The uncanny small sounds from way down the deep gully-course as it passes under Torrington Bridge. The sound of foul water trickling slowly along. And other sounds, that were like blurred noises in the head, that were not of water trickling.

The houses all with blank, gloomy faces. As though they held no secrets, and could tell nothing. And over all the terrifying stillness. And over that again the cold, unreckoning stars.

The night folded him about, and forgot him. The city like a great monster lay heavily on its side in uneasy slumber. The night and the darkness and the stillness laid on, and the jungle slept.

Except for the great cats that lurked, and sprang out, and took their victims unawares. The long cry of terror in the night. The long cry of pain. The tortured, drawn-out, strangled cry, as another victim feels the toothed death sharp as its vitals. The great cats prowling through this jungle of men.

Except for the dogs eternally scuffling among garbage for offal.

Better, he thought, to come a victim of one, of those great cats . . . jealously without pity . . . the clean sharp rip of stiletto going through yielding, unwilling flesh . . . anger and lust and greed and hate, without pity. The sharp tooth of death finding the quick release, the sudden dark end . . . like a sea of darkness and night without end . . . and the great downward determined plunge . . . down, down to dark eternity, to the black womb of endlessness again returning . . . to night and the black shining water under the firmament of stars.

Better to come a victim of one of the great cats, he thought, than to be dragged down by the mangey dogs.

So he took courage again, and smiled within himself, secretly. Keeping always to the middle of the road. He was drunk with the night and the thought of death.

Better to come in the darkness of the jungle upon the two great green eyes set wide apart. Or to feel the hot breath for an instant upon the neck, as the great cat leaps upon its kill.

The last long cry, strange and unutterably sad in its utter aloneness, as the sharp death reaches down, toothed and terrible, for the very quick of life . . . to pluck life up at the quick. To undo the knot. To release the pent-up dark stream of tremendous nothingness. Terror of the night translated to knowledge. Translated to triumph. To sudden release, that is the loosing of one hold to take everlasting hold upon another.

Better that, he mused, stumbling a little as he walked – as one who has come a great way – than to be pulled down by the foul and sulking dogs, to a more cruel and shameful end.

Upon the pavement in front of a Chinese shop a man slept. A blurred dark figure against the other darkness. A prowling dog dragged its pitiful body nearer and nosed the prone man.

He smiled deep down inside himself and took courage in the night again. And walked along, stumbling a little as he walked. But with great care, with an almost comical precision, a nice discrimination, keeping always to the middle of the road.

It was past three in the morning. Strange voices sang inside his head. He was walking home from a night of carousing.

His thoughts were overtaken by the darkness, and the gloominess, and the eeriness, and death. But his feet were taking him home.

The Tramp

Tramp, tramp, tramp the city over, sweat and sun, sun and the dust of highways taking all directions, going everywhere at once and getting you nowhere. The meaning of life, the meaning of direction, of process, lost in the ceaseless procession, the endless burden of footsteps. The greater, a man's soul, contained within the lesser, the sordidness of adjacents surrounding him; brick, and stucco buildings, and the hidden termite in the wall working its endless destruction in secret. Perishable taking its ceaseless spoil of imperishable. Hedged in on all sides by rotting walls, barbed wire, and the unsightliness of corrugated iron sheets.

Unless a man could lift himself up out of all this, and stride majestically across the rooftops of the world, there was no getting away from them. The Janes and the Thomases too. Most of all was a man's soul hedged about by them. You had to seek them out and sit with them, and take conversation to them as a means of making contact. And you found that you got nothing from all this. But what was still worse you could give nothing. It was like feeding upon yourself, eating your own flesh in secret.

Until at last despairing you reached for a bottle, for the antidote. Or staggered to bed with some Jane, for the antidote. Because a man is sick and afraid. Then he gets up again and takes his clothes, and stands upon his own feet again, and with himself – and alone and sick and afraid, eating his own flesh in secret.

Not the calendar, not the clock on the wall ticks off the measured units of a man's span upon earth. But black pints stood on end, rows of them, and the painted tarts. The Janes. These tell of his escapes, his releases, his casual partaking again and again of death, seeking otherness elsewhere. Not as the dial of the clock, for that tells nothing. Another blank face, like this Jane and the last, and the first; no heart, no mind, no real contact anywhere. Alien surfaces discovering their infinities, but no comprehension anywhere. And no cohesion.

He could close his eyes and see the slow, unceasing termite-destruction keeping pace with the other, everywhere. Everywhere coming to dust in secret, in darkness coming to death. And on the surface only everything carrying on just the same, smiling, debonair, carrying within it the substance and the sentence of death. He could close his eyes tight and see it the same everywhere. The little laughing tart, taking avidly with her hands with the painted fingernails, taking to herself the endless nothing, bestowing nothing again, eating her own life in secret. But on the surface painted, smiling, false, the same.

It troubled him that despite himself he could give nothing of himself, bestow nothing anywhere. He saw himself a fruit hanging from its branch in ripeness and in richness, and in readiness. But unable to fall away, to make the necessary sacrifice, the separation, to make way for eternal fruition and newness, renewing himself again and again. Himself a ripe fruit coming to flux on the branch. The worm eating away in secret under the skin.

Himself and this Jane, sharing the same banalities, the same bed, but as far removed from each other as though divided by oceans and continents, living on different planes of consciousness, aware through different stimuli of the same to by four of habitable hell.

And yet this was not all. Somewhere again there existed the common denominator that must make each acceptable to the other, and related to all the rest.

The party at Jake's last week. The gramophone music and the shuffling hips. There was richness in that and freedom in that. People letting go of their inhibitions and laughing and coming alive. But you couldn't take anything of that away with you. Because that was only an escape. A means to an end. And he could hardly blame the people who had come to regard the means as an end in itself. The unrest everywhere. The world busying itself with all the known antidotes to boredom. People asking to be made happy. To find happiness here ready-made for them. Or else finding it in non-resistance to inertia. Making the higher reaches of their minds inaccessible to them, and accepting this kind of semi-insensibility as a way of living, because they are afraid of process, that is pain, that is inseparable from growth.

The bottle-party at Jake's last week was rated a great success, because nobody got so drunk as to misbehave himself. Or stayed so sober as to forget they had come here to be happy for a night, to be boys and girls together in the way of bright young people taking a fling at living.

But you couldn't take any part of Jake's party under your vest home. You couldn't take away anything but a headache and a bad taste in your mouth the morning after. And that was the hell of it. That was life saying to every man and woman of them, you didn't come here to appropriate to yourself large helpings of happiness, but to learn about process, and through pain, and to make death a splendid thing, beautiful with giving, which is the whole purpose of life.

What troubled him now wasn't at all that he too suffered this negation with the rest, but that he was unable to give. He was bursting with the gift, love, joy, and the wholeness of involuntary process, but nowhere to bestow it.

Tramp, tramp, tramp, from one point to another. Taking the dust of the city and the heat and the glare of the sun and the irritation everywhere, going from one place to another. Exchanging greetings with the rest, each going the same, taking all directions, to the last.

And so he walked until he came to a time and a place. And he stood still in the present letting go of everything. The time and the place, and the process of getting here. Loosing the knots, the enigma, the paradox, the irritation, all attitudes but at last the one, the utterly receptive.

And the light broke about his head, and he took it in his hands and whirled and whirled it round until it formed itself into a loop for him to stand in, nowhere and, out of time, on an elevation that was like a hill. At the centre of all, of endlessness and nothing, he stood upon that elevation, within the circle of light.

He saw the first peep of the bud on a green twig, saw it taking light from the source the sun and weaving it into a pattern. Uttering out of the joy at the core of it, the centre of creation, the pure aesthetic substance of its being, and understood it for all it was, song and process, and the embodiment of joy and pain. But always proceeding from joy, the song, the eternal, and through pain the process, on to joy again, and each moment of the way, endlessly, even to death and beyond . . . always the song, always with singing, the same and changing through all variations and interpretations and shades, of meaning, to song again at the putting-forth, the beginning.

And as well understood it within himself, joy working its divine will and eternal through process and pain, and proceeding in this manner to death and perpetual newness in the womb, the end and the beginning from everlasting to everlasting.

And Jane lying in her little painted leaf of a couch the same, taking her place in the procession, changing, changing, as the song changes on the singer's lips, forming its pattern of wholeness and beauty.

Coming at last to this time and place, that is nowhere and now, he discovered himself the instrument of that song at the lips of that singer . . . and a tramp in the midst of houses and men and interminable streets that lead everywhere.

Tramp, tramp, tramp . . . sweat and sun . . . sun and the dust of highways taking all directions . . . the houses standing in their green plots, the hedges and the iron fences and barbed wire, and beyond the termite-riddled walls . . . this avenue and the next the same, and all ways and all directions the same . . . tramp, tramp, tramp, and the twilight closing in upon all. And hunger that is the sign of a healthy appetite, and the longing for human contacts again. And now almost within reach of the means to allay them, almost home.

Part II

The Crooked Branch

ALTHOUGH the boy occupied the position of a menial in the household, having been adopted at an early age, there was a certain freedom, not to say familiarity, between himself and the other members of the family. He was on occasions allowed to join in their games when the children needed a fourth, but as he was nearly two years older than the eldest, Charles, and was always better than the others at most games, they gradually dropped out of the practice of having him along as a matter of course; unless they needed him to make an even number.

The two little girls, Flossie and Junie, chatted and told lies, and once when Caleb, horrified, had threatened to tell on them, they made up a story to take to their parents about his having taken a switch to them, which earned for Caleb a sound thrashing at the hands of their father, after their mother had reported the matter to him on his return from office that day.

It must be said, however, that only rarely did such a thing happen, and only for a really serious offence. Like that time when Caleb had blacked Charles' eye for him, because of a quarrel they had had over a bird's next Caleb had found in a guinep tree. Charles wanted to take the eggs and Caleb wouldn't let him. But Charles thought he would be blowed if he would allow himself to be bossed by Caleb who was little better than a garden boy, although he enjoyed certain privileges. Children are not slow in observing certain things, and although there was never any overt action on the part of either Mr or Mrs Pepper to show there was any difference between them, they jolly well knew that there was just the same. It was just there, for all that. And so there was nothing for it but for Caleb to do what he did. He wasn't a bit repentant for having

16

blacked his eye for Charles. And he didn't think anything of the licking he had had to take for doing it, either. It was inevitable, all that had happened. And Caleb was never one for harbouring any too rosy illusions about life. After all, Charles was Charles. He couldn't expect to go blacking the eye of Mrs Pepper's boy, and not catch it. But he would be the last person to say that either Mr or Mrs Pepper had ever been anything but kind to him in all the years he lived with them.

When Flossie and Junie were fourteen and twelve respectively they had a party to which they invited a number of their schoolfriends. It was a party to celebrate the end of the Summer term and the beginning of the long holiday. Charles at this time was going to a boarding school for boys. Some of their guests, in particular a little flaxen-haired girl of about Junie's age, named Marjorie, were horrified to hear Caleb, whom they designated as 'the garden boy', addressing Flossie and Junie by their first names, without any prefix. The boy had been enlisted on this occasion because he was the only one available to hold one end of a long skipping rope, while six little girls played a sort of skipping game that was very popular with them.

That night Flossie put the matter squarely to her mother; about Caleb calling them by their first names, plain.

'He is not the same as us, is he, Mother? He is our garden boy, isn't he?' said Flossie.

'Well, yes dear. I'll speak to him about it first thing in the morning. But you must be kind to him always, remember. We adopted him when he was quite a little chap, that was before any of you was born. He has grown up to consider himself almost one of the family. You must never forget that. And none of my children must ever, ever be unkind to Caleb.'

The following morning when Caleb came in to get the girls' shoes that they were going to wear to school, to clean them, Flossie was only just awake.

'Who is that?' said she, sitting up, and rubbing the sleep out of her eyes.

'Hello,' said Caleb, grinning. 'How come you're awake so soon?'

'Did you knock before you came in?' said Flossie looking at him unsmilingly. 'Don't you know you should knock before you enter a lady's room?'

The boy looked at her with laughter in his eyes.

'Yes, Ma'm,' he said, mockingly.

Her hair falling down the front of her nightdress gave her an angelic look that seemed to belie the temper of her.

'Now get out,' she said. And when he didn't move. 'Did you hear me? Get out. I want to dress.'

Junie, in her own little bed, turned over on her side and opened her eyes.

'What's the matter?' she said, pettishly. 'You woke me up.'

'It's time to get up, anyhow,' said Flossie, sharply.

'It's not, either. And you don't try to boss me about as you please. I'll tell Papa.'

'Why don't you girls stop wrangling and go back to sleep. You got another good ten minutes left. The bath won't be free for that time, anyway,' said Caleb.

'Who asked your opinion?' Flossie said.

'Shut up, Flossie,' said Junie.

'Don't pay any attention to her, Junie. She woke up on her wrong side, that's all,' the boy said.

'Who are you calling Junie, Flossie, like that?' cried the elder girl with indignation. 'Mama says you are to say Miss to us. And if you don't you'll see what happens.'

'Say *Miss*? What you mean?'

'I'm not going to have any argument with you about it. You may go now,' said Flossie, with great dignity.

After breakfast, when the two girls had gone to town to do some shopping for themselves, and Papa had left for office, Mama called Caleb to her and talked to him kindly but firmly. She explained that the social position of her children warranted him calling them Miss Flossie and Miss Junie, and Mr Charles. It took nothing from him to be polite to people, she said. She didn't want him to think that anything was meant by it; that is, no one wished to belittle him in any way, but she had to think of the social position of her children. Other children had noticed it, and remarked upon it. She was sure he for one wouldn't want their schoolmates to think the less of them; Mr Charles, and Miss Flossie, and Miss Junie. Nobody wished to be unkind to him, least of all herself, he knew that. But she would have to insist upon this.

Caleb said nothing, but that afternoon when Mr Pepper came home from office he went to him and without giving any reason told him that he was going to leave. There was some money belonging to him in the post office bank, that had been saved there for him and Mr Pepper kept the passbook. He would like to draw it out because he was going away.

'Going away?' said Mr Pepper, frowning. 'Whatever made you come to this sudden decision?'

Caleb told him.

'It's not that I think myself too good to do as Mrs Pepper wants, but I don't like it,' he said. 'I feel there is something behind it all, and I don't like it. So I'm leaving, Sir, that's all.'

'But this is ridiculous, Caleb. You can't leave on account of that. Besides why was I never told anything about this. I assure you my boy I knew nothing of it whatever. You wait here. I guess I have something to say about all this.'

But some time later when Mr Pepper called him to talk it over, he seemed to have modified his views somewhat. He begged Caleb not to act rashly. He would be sorry for him to go. After all he had tried all these years always to do the right thing by him, and this was hardly the way to repay him, them, for all they had done for him. After all it was a little thing, and he was sure Caleb would reconsider it, in a different light, and take a saner view of the manner.

After that Caleb went off by himself for a long walk. He did not return for supper, and it was not until the household had retired for the night that he slunk in as though he was afraid of being seen, and went to bed in the little room just off the back verandah which he occupied.

After that he didn't talk about leaving any more. He just went about his work the same, but with a quiet, subdued air now, rarely smiling or saying anything, unless he was directly addressed.

One day it happened that Junie saw him sitting in the swing in the garden. Just sitting, not doing anything, and she came up to him, feeling somehow pained because of the way he looked, so lonely and unhappy.

'Why are you sitting there?' she said.

And when he got up immediately and walked away without saying anything, it hurt her all the more. She was sorry she had spoken to him. It was as though her very presence had scared him away. And she felt so hurt because of the deep hurt that she divined in him, that she wanted to cry, herself.

There were certain differences between himself and the other children that Caleb began to notice now for the first time. Such as the fact that his skin was somewhat darker than theirs, and his hair more curly. And these things began to take on a certain significance in his mind, albeit almost unconsciously.

When Charles came home for the summer holidays, there was no one at home that afternoon but Caleb.

Caleb took his grips inside, and when Charles said.

'Well Caleb, boy, how's everything,' he was surprised that all he got from the other was a sort of grunt.

'Come on an' help me open up this grip, inside,' said Charles. 'Boy, I've gotta bat for a prize! A genuine George Headley willow. Second eleven, you know. I'm captain of the second now. Didn't you know?'

'Yes, Mr Charles,' said Caleb. 'I did hear some talk about it.'

Charles just opened his eyes a little wider and stared at him. But he didn't say anything.

Something happened then, though, in that instant, that was to last for a lifetime. And it was this, simply.

Caleb said, with a sudden warmth for this boy who had been his playmate all these years, and remembering it was he who had first coached him in batting, teaching him all the strokes, the cuts, the drives, how to pivot and slice a ball to leg, and how to step out and deal with a Yorker; and with pride in his voice:

'Gee, that's wonderful! About your making top score, and winning the cup for your school. It was you who did it. I heard the folks talking about it.'

And Charles just looked at him, as though a great gulf had suddenly opened between them, that could never be bridged.

20

'Oh, yes,' said Charles.

And he started to unpack the grip slowly, and without any special enthusiasm now, as though he had forgotten what it had been all about.

When Flossie was seventeen she left school and went to work in her father's office as cashier, or something. But what was more important still, she had her first real boy friend. She brought him home and introduced him to the family.

Jerry himself was only nineteen, but he drove home with Flossie in a swanky yellow coupé that had been given him by his father for his very own.

As he opened the door Flossie sprang out with a gay little laugh, and went in through the gate. Caleb was just standing by idly looking on, with that lost look in his face that had become fixed there now for good, a kind of abstraction that made him look as though he were not all there.

Jerry came in through the gate after her, his hands full of all sorts of feminine things, like Flossie's wrap and handbag and parcels of all sizes and descriptions.

'Here, boy,' he said to Caleb, giving over some of the parcels into his hands.

Flossie laughed.

'Come on, Jerry. Hurry. I'm just dying to open the little one. Here, give it me.'

Both Flossie and Junie had grown quite exceptionally pretty. Flossie in a slender, vivacious, and even imperious way; and Junie all soft round curves, ripening out almost too soon, giving her an appearance of being much older than her years. More lately too something of the sweetness and gentleness of her expression had given way to a sullen sort of loveliness, that went with her indolent disposition.

Junie had started to have rows with her parents already, because she wanted to leave school and go get a job for herself, like other girls of her age had done. But they would have none of it.

Another time she had had an important row with her mother on account of a certain red-haired youth who used to visit her regularly. In fact they belonged to the same gang. The gang numbered about thirty. Boys and girls all of school age. They went out cycling, sea-bathing, hiking, picnicking together. Nearly every afternoon they went out somewhere; if not all the gang, at least some of them. Sometimes they would leave home on a Saturday morning and not return until nine or ten at night; when Junie would be so tired out from her exertions that she would tumble into bed fully dressed, just kicking off her shoes, and fall asleep like that, without waking again until next morning.

This went on for many months until one day Mrs Pepper suddenly decided to put her foot down on Junie carrying on like that. There was a most terrific row, in which Junie threatened to do all sorts of dreadful things if they didn't let her alone, and was in turn threatened with being banished to some desolate part of the country where her uncle Ben had a banana property.

There was not much love lost between the sisters, either. Flossie never ceased to try to boss Junie, and Junie never tired of showing her contempt for Flossie.

The first time Jerry came to the house they had a row at tea.

'I wish you wouldn't say 'gee' about every two sentences, like that,' said Junie to her elder sister. 'It sounds so dreadfully vulgar and affected.'

'Indeed,' said Flossie, bridling and on her dignity. 'Perhaps it wouldn't be out of place for you to mind your own business either, I should say.'

And so on and so forth. Until Flossie retired to her room – they had separate bedrooms now that Charles had gone to England to university – with a terrific headache, right after Jerry left. And Junie went about the house whistling triumphantly, and wound up by having a row with the cook over some scones, that hadn't been ready in time for tea, and that Junie was greedily stuffing herself with now.

'You'll soon be fat as a little pig,' said Cookie, 'if you keep up stuffing all the time like that.' Because she knew that her tendency to run to flesh was even at this early age a matter of grave concern to the girl.

It was about this time that Mr Pepper called Caleb to him one day and had a good heart-to-heart talk with him.

What Mr Pepper said was, now that Caleb was a young man perhaps it was time for him to think about going out into the world and trying to better his position. The money he had saved in the bank amounted to almost thirty pounds. Mr Pepper would give him another thirty on top of that, and he should try to set himself up in some sort of business in a small way.

As far as Caleb's education was concerned he could read and write and cipher. That was about all. The fact is that he and Charles had gone to the same school when they were little boys and Caleb had shown such brilliance at his studies that in a couple of years he was way ahead of Charles, and seeing that his progress was so rapid it was thought just as well to take him out of school now, because he had learnt quite as much as it was necessary for him to get along in the world. So Mrs Pepper had told him, and he had not thought to offer any opposition to the suggestion.

There was the lawn to be mowed, so Caleb mowed the lawn instead of going to school one day. And then there was always one thing or another to be done about the house, or in the yard, or the garden. And Caleb just did what he was told to do. For one thing he had come to realise from quite early in life that Mr and Mrs Pepper were not really his parents. They had only adopted him. Just how it had happened, that is how he came to be adopted by them, and who his real parents were, remained a complete mystery to him all his life, and he was never encouraged to ask questions about it. Gradually he grew up to think there must have been something not quite respectable about his mother, and as far as his father was concerned he seemed to be a sort of mythical person who never had any real substantial existence at all.

He understood that these people had been more than kind in adopting him, and taking care of him all these years, and that he owed them a debt of gratitude that could not be easily repaid. Consequently when it was brought to his notice that there were things to be done, he just did them, as though nothing was more natural in the world than that these tasks should fall to his lot. For instance, when he no longer had to go to school, what was more natural than he should take the other childrens' shoes early in the morning into the pantry and sit on a stool and clean them, so that they would have time to do the home lessons they had not managed to get through the evening before.

But now, as Mr Pepper tried to show him, he had grown a young man, and it was time for him to think of making something of his life. But Caleb just couldn't conceive of any sort of life other than this, here. Here was his life. His security, his bread and butter and bed, were here. That was how he had come to regard it all these years. He felt there was nowhere for him to go. There was nothing for him to do. Still if they insisted, he would just have to go, that was all.

'Not at all,' Mr Pepper said, quickly. 'We are thinking only of your good, Caleb. Anyway, there is no immediate hurry, you understand. We don't want you to feel as though we have become tired of you, and are pushing you out into the world and cutting you adrift. But think it over, all the same.'

And Caleb did, but still he could come to no decision. Frankly he was frightened of the prospect of being cut adrift to make shift for himself in a cold and hostile world. So after a bit he just ceased to think of it any more, and remained on.

And so it was that another year passed and Caleb was still there.

But several changes had taken place in the meantime. For one thing Flossie had a birthday party when she was nineteen, and she invited a whole host of friends to dance and play games and eat ice cream and cake. And besides there was a large bowl of rum punch.

The party was a very merry, and even boisterous one. That is, it started to get boisterous about three o'clock in the morning.

After the guests had all gone home he was property tired, because he had had plenty of work to do serving them, dressed up for the occasion in an old suit that had belonged to Charles, and a pair of Mr Pepper's boots that creaked when he walked, and caused the young people no end of amusement.

He had had only about four or five rum punches himself, that he had snatched up and poured down his throat hastily in the pantry. But they must have been large ones, for when he sat on the edge of his bed and tried to pull off his boots his head felt all funny inside as though it was going round and round. He had to sit upright again suddenly to prevent himself falling all in a heap on the floor.

He felt curiously happy inside him though. And he started remembering many things that had happened during the course of the night that now made him laugh.

He remembered Jerry taking Flossie's glass from her and showing them a balancing trick that ended up with his getting all the liquor down the front of his dress shirt, while the others screamed with laughter.

They had supper served buffet style. He remembered a young man saying to Junie, who was flushed and gay, and more lovely in her soft round indolent way than he had ever seen her: 'Have a pea, Junie?'

And she holding on to his arm and laughing up into his face. 'Not just now, I think, Hal!'

At which they had both laughed some more.

He remembered how Junie's warm glance had fallen upon him another time, catching him unawares, as it were. And how it warmed him to see her looking at him like that. It was as though the warmth had been there in her eyes all along, and she had just turned her gaze upon him for an instant, forgetting that he was not one of the guests. Perhaps it was on account of the suit he was wearing, Charles' suit. Flossie he remembered had demurred somewhat about having him come among her guests dressed in Charles' cast-off suit. She had feared it might cause no end of embarrassment. But it hadn't.

And he was glad, because Junie had looked at him like that. Suddenly he realized that he was tremendously happy about it.

He was laying across the bed and thinking about these things and feeling curiously happy inside when she appeared before him there in the open doorway. She was wearing a kimono, and he thought he had never seen anyone so beautiful in all his life before.

It is true he still went in and out of their rooms, as the occasion warranted, and he had seen both girls in various stages of undress: because they had grown so used to having him about that they didn't pay any mind to him. Besides he was – well, he. That is to say he wasn't exactly a servant, and at the same time he wasn't one of them. And all the time he had never taken any particular notice.

But now, seeing her standing there, he was seeing her in a new light altogether.

'Aren't you gone to bed yet?' she said, coming into the room. 'I can't sleep, either. Isn't it odd that both of us should be like that?' She gave an odd little laugh. 'I feel all restless inside. Have you ever felt that way?'

It seemed the most natural thing in the world that she should be here talking to him. Neither she nor Flossie thought twice about entering his room, if they wanted him for something special, like mending a shoe heel that had come off, or fixing the connection of a bicycle pump that had somehow come undone, things like that. It was something they had always done. And somehow, that it was past four in the morning, it didn't seem to make any difference to his pleasantly befuddled mind.

She was looking at him with that same warm light in her eyes. And laughing he reached up and took her face between his hands, as though he were shielding a tiny flame against the wind.

And she was leaning toward him, unresisting, her lips slightly parted.

It was not until the next morning that the full realization came to him, of all that had happened to him during the night. He realized that he was in love – with Junie! And that she loved him with that same wonderful meaning he never for a moment doubted.

This thing was too big for him to contain, he felt. In his simple way he thought that he must tell someone about it. And who better to tell about it than his guardian, the man who had adopted him and brought him up almost like a son, out of the bigness of his heart.

And so he went to Mr Pepper and told him quite simply of his love for Junie. And when the man in a sort of horrified whisper sought to drag the whole story out of him in a series of rather blunt questions that made the boy pained and ashamed, he told him that he would have to leave this place that he had come to regard as home, right away. He must go, today, now.

He would not even let him see Junie. No, he would explain everything to her. He must leave it to him. But on no account was he ever to breathe a word of this to anyone, *anyone*.

He would see what he could do about fixing it with a friend of his in some distant country town to take him into his shop and teach him the business from the ground up. Later he could open a small provision shop of his own and make something of himself.

But he must never think of Junie again. This thing was quite impossible. He must never try to communicate with her in any way, or ever try to see her again.

The boy just listened to him in that dull uncomprehending silence that had become habitual with him now; with that same stupid look of abstraction, as though he were not altogether there.

'There is something I ought to tell you,' said Mr Pepper. And then he seemed to change his mind. 'Never mind . . . perhaps . . . perhaps some day . . .'

What good would it do, he thought, to tell him the truth, that he and Junie were half-brother and half-sister. Better not, he decided; the boy would obey him implicitly, he knew. He would go away – never try to see her or communicate with her again.

Perhaps it was even consideration for his feelings that made Mr Pepper determine to keep the secret.

What was the sense hurting him more than he need be hurt. Destroying once and for all for him what was perhaps the one wholly beautiful thing in life that he had ever known.

The Little Cobbler

THE little shop at the corner of the lane, by an odd trick of architecture, turned a cold shoulder to High Street. At least it feigned the cold shoulder by presenting to the main thoroughfare a blank whitewashed wall. Had it not done so the rental for so much floor space on an important street like that would have placed it altogether beyond the little cobbler's slender means.

This ridiculous little hole-in-the-wall, hobnobbing with a large general store on one side and a shirt factory on the other, was the cause of the strange friendship between that oddly assorted pair, Pinero, the Cuban proprietor of the shirt factory, and Zaccy (for short), the little cobbler himself. The shop looked like a side pocket of the store premises, and its sign, 'The Shoe Factory', impudently mimicked the shirt factory's that bravely fronted the High Street.

As to the old cobbler himself, he wore a pair of spectacles perched on top of his forehead, and a round, inquisitive face that was as impudent as the sign above his shop door, and the colour of the leather he used in resoling the shoes of his customers. But the impudence of his sign was not directed at the shirt factory. From where he sat on the pavement just outside his door, Zaccy could see the sign of the 'Electric Shoe Repair Shop', in neon-lights fronting the broad thoroughfare. Indeed, without moving his stool he could read the PAIR SHOP part of it. The idea of his large rival calling his establishment a 'shop' with artistic understatement, prompted him to adopt the still more naive overstatement of 'Shoe Factory' for his modest place.

He had never met the proprietor of the Shoe Shop, but he knew the man was a prosperous Cuban, as was also the proprietor of the shirt factory. He had talked with the latter often, in the hope of learning something about the former, but he was not for giving away secrets to the enemy. Still Zaccy liked the man, and sometimes, after he had closed his shop, he would stroll across to the business office of his neighbour and discuss with him the topics of the day.

Pinero was a tactful man who had no enemies, since he preferred to regard every man as his friend. When Zaccy would complain of the artfulness of the Shoe Shop man in attracting business to his place by such subterfuges as giving away free bottles of shoe-whiting – and lately had added a hat-cleaning department – Pinero just sat back in his swivel-chair and roared heartily, slapping his fat thighs.

'He de smart chap, eh? He tek de trade away from you, don't it? Why you don' t'ink up somet'ing too, to tek de trade away from he?'

But Zaccy believed in honest, four-square business principles. No giving away of premiums to customers for him. No sir. The public was pampered enough as it was. Nowadays a man didn't buy a packet of cigarettes unless there was a chance of finding a 'valuable coupon' inside. Proprietory articles, from condensed milk to floor polish, from chewing-gum to soap tablets, were sold, not on the quality of the products, but on the value of the premiums given away 'free' with so many labels. It made the old cobbler snort with disgust.

In answer to a direct question from the other, Pinero shook his head and said: 'Yes, he good fren' of mine – but I no tell his name. Ver', ver' good fren' – de bes'! You like heem too, if you know heem. He have de good heart underneat', but de skin of heem is t'ick, ver' t'ick!' He exploded into a gust of laughter, his round face becoming a bright cherry-red underneath the tan, and damp with perspiration.

'Ef I had de bis'nis of you,' Pinero said, seriously, 'I would not watch dis fellow. I would stay in my shop an' be glad t'inkin' of de expense of he, kippin' up dat show . . . Myself, I kip awake in de night while you mek de snore, t'inkin' about one beeg overdraft at de bank, he could float a warship. Pretty soon, mebbe, me an' he monkey in de same cage, eh?'

But Zaccy found small comfort in these negative considerations.

On the other hand it never occurred to him that while the other prospered and expanded from month to month, from year to year, his own small business remained the same, his income never fluctuating any month by so much as a pound note. It never occurred to him that he was quite comfortably off, in fact, from any point of view, in that his income exceeded his expenditure by a margin large enough to permit him to put aside something in the Government Savings Bank every week. And he stinted himself of nothing. He ate the best food always – square, nourishing meals in a restaurant to his liking – dingy it was, and cheap looking, it is true – but there he found himself among congenial company, where his opinions on the current topics of the day were held in something of respect, and even awe, by the other customers.

He owed no money. He had no responsibilities. He still kept his old customers from year to year, gossiping with them as they waited while he put the finishing touches to the jobs that he always delivered on time. Indeed, it would seem that life was particularly uneventful and uninspiring for Zaccy because the one fly in his pot of ointment was the Shoe Shop across the way.

And so it would have been to the end of his days, but Zaccy must needs fall ill suddenly. His illness was a serious one, too, and there was a time when they feared for his life. But he was a tough old man, and bit by bit he mended, with a stubbornness that was typical.

Pinero came to see him at the hospital every week – sometimes twice, or even three times in a week, bringing him little gifts and sitting by his bedside and chatting with him. On one occasion he brought a mysterious looking box which he bade the old man open himself. He stood aside and watched with glistening eyes full of fun and mischief as Zaccy undid the strings and the paper wrappings, lifted the lid; and then looked so crestfallen and defeated as the other peered into the box near-sightedly to see what strange, mysterious gift lay therein, among the tissue paper.

'Mebbe he ketch de sick heemself, eh?' said Pinero, reaching out a hand to take the package from the other, 'But I fix heem quick.'

And even as he took the box in his hand something leaped out of it straight at Zaccy's face. Zaccy gave a shriek, and sick as he was he nearly leapt from the bed, while Pinero sat beside him and roared himself red in the face, smacking his fat thighs and rocking backwards and forwards.

The commotion brought Nurse hurrying to Zaccy's bedside. It took all of Pinero's tact to get around her after that. She was thoroughly mad at him for having upset the patient, and causing such a disturbance in her ward.

But the fat little man, having retrieved the box, proceeded to demonstrate the strange contraption to her, while Zaccy watched the operation, a little fearfully at first, from the bed. The box contained a small metal toad, painted green. When the lid was removed, a spring was immediately released (unless something went wrong, which it appears was sometimes the case), and the toad jumped out of the box in a most realistic manner.

As he made the toad jump again Pinero let out a little peal of triumphant laughter and handed it to the nurse.

'Here, you mek heem joomp. He can' bite . . . he can' hurt you wort' a dam.'

But Nurse was not easily mollified. She bundled him quickly out of the ward to the general merriment of the occupants.

At the door Pinero paused, straw hat in hand, an apologetic smile upon his red, perspiring face. He winked with great unction at the nurse who tried to preserve a severe appearance.

'I t'ink heem do he good, mebbe,' he confided. 'Pretty soon mek he joomp too, eh? Den he get well agan! He, ha, ha!' He exploded two or three times again before he reached the bottom of the stairs.

Zaccy spent altogether ten months at the hospital. Towards the end he became more and more depressed. Pinero still came to see him regularly, bringing him as usual little gifts of candy, fruit, and sometimes even flowers. He brought with him his small daughter, aged seven, to present the flowers to his sick friend. She was a beautiful child with large eyes and a wonderful, fleeting smile.

'I bring Angella to spik to you, Senor,' he said. 'Spik to de Senor, Angella mia. She spik de Engleesh,' he told Nurse, proudly, bunching up his fingers and kissing the tips of them to the ceiling. 'Spik to de Senorita, pepita mia.'

Angella smiled, bowed, and said, 'Good morning,' very correctly.

'We don't spik about de bis'nis now,' he remonstrated firmly with Zaccy when the other asked how things were getting on at the Shoe Factory. 'When you okay agen we spik about de bis'nis, eh? You get better queek, queek time an' we spik about de bis'nis den.'

But Zaccy was worried. His savings was very nearly all gone now. He was a paying-patient at the hospital. He had undergone four different operations, had had to be put on a special diet, and the extras for special nourishment, tonics, etc, mounted up to something colossal.

The day that he was well enough to leave the hospital Pinero called for him in his own luxurious closed car, with Angella and a chauffeur. This day, Pinero announced, they would celebrate.

Zaccy wanted to be taken straight to the Shoe Factory, but Pinero would not hear of it. There was plenty of time for that yet. Today they would go into the country to a little place he knew of where it was all green pastures and verdant fields, with real mountains of deep blue beyond.

They would show Zaccy how Angella could milk a cow. They would remain there a week, two weeks maybe. So Zaccy for all his impatience, had to bide his time, for Pinero was in command.

Soon surprising changes began to appear on the countenances of both men, for as Zaccy's became more and more that of a man who is without a care in the world, and comfortably off, Pinero's became graver, and his manner quieter and more thoughtful each day.

Zaccy felt he would never forget all this as long as he lived. He felt ashamed, now that he had time to think of it, that he had really done so little to deserve all this. Pinero's friendship suddenly became something to be valued above gold, and as for little Angella, they became closer and closer as the days went by. She gradually lost all her shyness of him as she grew to know him better, and would sit on his knee while he told her all the Anancy stories he could remember. To him she was just a lovely little angel, indeed – and he had not a care in the world.

They would be returning to the city the day after tomorrow, and Pinero realized he could keep the bad news no longer from his friend. And so he told him bluntly now what he had kept carefully hidden hidden from him all these months. How his old customers and friends had one by one ceased to go to the Shoe Factory with their repair jobs, although Pinero had, at his own expense, installed an electric shoe repairing machine, and an expert to operate it, in the premises. How one after the other both Zaccy's assistants had left. How things had gone steadily from bad to worse, until there had not been enough money even to pay the rental of the premises.

But it would be all right, everything would be the same as usual when Zaccy returned. His old customers would come back to him. One by one they would find him again.

But Zaccy shook his head. Suddenly he felt very old. He knew he would never be able to build up the business he had had before. The Electric Shoe Shop across the way would have the trade, the custom – all that had ever come to him. He would never be able to get them back. He bowed his face in his hands, and the tears trickled between his fingers. Pinero laid a fat hand upon his shoulder, but said nothing. For once in his life he was bereft of words. Suddenly he felt himself out of place here, impotent, an interloper. With a dejected shrug of his shoulders he moved away.

He would offer the old man a job in his Electric Shoe Repair Shop, but it would be like adding insult to injury. Would not Zaccy see at the bottom of it a malicious subterfuge to deprive him of his independence – just another deep scheme on the part of an unscrupulous competitor?

The following week Zaccy went back to the Shoe Factory. Apart from the fact that he was a little thinner, a little greyer, and consequently his face a little less impudent in appearance, his manner a little less dogmatic, assured, he was the same old Zaccy. Once in a while an old friend would stop and pass the time of day, but mostly they passed on the other side of the High Street now, or even walked the length of a whole block to avoid him, as though ashamed to meet his eye.

He kept up the appearance for a few months, and then one afternoon, after he had a long gossip with an old crony who had happened along he shut up his shop and took down his sign. He went across to the shirt factory and asked if Pinero was in his office. Pinero himself came out to him. He had caught sight of him through the window coming in by the street entrance.

'A-a-a-ah, my friend,' exclaimed he, jovially. 'Come in, come in an' mek yourself de home. I hear de news from you, eh? A long time I have not see you, eh?'

Zaccy came in slowly, without saying a word. Pinero read his face and he knew that the other had at last made his momentous discovery.

Still without saying a word the old man laid the sign on the floor against the wall, the lettered side out, where Pinero could not help seeing it from across his desk. Then he came close up to the desk and resting the tips of his fingers upon the shining mahogany, leaned forward and spoke in a voice that trembled.

'Snake!' he hissed. 'Dam snake, pretending all the time you was my friend, while you turn around like the snake you are, and wriggle and squirm until you done me out of my business.' He paused to draw breath. The blood underneath his fingernails showed purple, Pinero observed, without knowing why his mind should be occupied at that moment with such seemingly trivial details. 'You have been very kind to me, *Mister* Pinero. Oh, very, very kind. I want not to seem to be ungrateful for all you have done, so I have brought you that . . .' Pointing to the sign. 'It's a little souvenir from me to you. When you look at it you will remember an old man, maybe, who you have done out of his living, with your smooth, oily ways.' He turned, and before Pinero could say a word, he had gone, closing the door quietly behind him.

Pinero stood at the window for a long time watching the shrunken figure of his friend go wearily down the street, until he became lost among the busy crowd . . . Oddly enough the picture of a sea came to his mind . . . the waves of this sea were human beings — men, and women, and children – and of a chip afloat upon this sea, being tossed about from wave to wave, seemingly without plan or purpose . . .

He wanted to run after that hopeless, broken figure, to take him by the arm, to pull him back to a place of security, to talk to him, to reason with him, to tell him of things he himself had never guessed at before, but knew now, intuitively, as with a flash of inspiration. But he knew that he dared not, that he had no place there beside that derelict chip of humanity. In the other's world of ideas he would be an interloper, a vulgar intruder . . . Between them there could be no reconciliation of ideas or ideals . . .

The man at the window knew all this in a sudden illuminating instant, that came and went.

He turned from the window with a shrug of his plump shoulders.

Black Magic

THE DAILY newspaper merely gave a brief account of how the body of a man had been found hanging from a tree by the outskirts of a popular city race track. It certainly did not mention that the body was that of an emaciated starved human wretch. But the man's name was given as Joe Smith, and a dramatic touch was added by the simple statement that a lady's handbag had been found in some bushes in the vicinity.

Over cocktails that same afternoon Ruth Marchmant was explaining to a bevy of excited young people of around her own age how her handbag had come to figure in a suicide case. When you stopped to think of it it was all so prosaic and unexciting. But for the moment it put her in the limelight, and she was enjoying it.

She had been trying to improve her putt on the golf course near the race track and had twisted her ankle. There was not a soul in sight and she had actually started to limp painfully toward the place where her car was parked when she saw this dried-up-looking black man coming towards her. He was playing mournfully upon a mouth organ, she remembered. Without a word he came to her assistance.

'Take it easy, Ma'am,' he said, and made her rest an arm upon his shoulder.

When she had got safely to the car, she had naturally asked his name.

'People call me Sandy. But me name Joe Smith,' he said. But he gravely and politely refused to take money from her. He looked hungry, too. Hungry, and haunted, and rather pathetic, the poor thing!

Just as she was about to drive away he stopped her.

'Ah know yuh is a sportin' lady,' he said, 'Ah always see yuh at de races. You gwine Sat'day, Ma'am?'

She nodded. He came closer. He looked about him as though to make certain there was no one listening.

'Buy 'Black Magic' to win in de t'ird race,' he whispered hoarsely in her ear. He looked at her quizzically as though to see if she understood. His excitement, his queerness, and a sort of reticence about him intrigued her.

She thought no more about it until Saturday when she saw him at the race track. He limped towards her, looking around him suspiciously as though he expected someone to come up and pinch him any moment.

''Member, ''Black Magic'' . . .!' he said in a husky undertone in passing, without looking at her.

She had to run after him and grab him by the arm, so quickly he limped away. But she just had to. The man, with his air of queerness, mystery, whatnot, was positively fascinating. She made no bones about it. She wanted to find out all she could about him. She questioned him.

She learnt that he was once a jockey. That he had been wrongfully suspended, according to his rather garbled account of it. Anyway it all had to do with obeah. Someone had 'set duppy on him'. Although he knew all the horses by their first names, and could pick winners in his sleep, not one of his bets came off now. Not once did his horse come anywhere near the winning post in company with the first three even. There was someone who hated him and set obeah on him. That was why he had given her 'Black Magic'. 'Black Magic' was almost a rank outsider. Yet he knew in some uncanny way that she would win. If she won, he hoped that she would remember him – remember that it was he who had helped her the other day, that it was he had given her the tip about 'Black Magic'.

No, he hadn't eaten, hardly for days, but that didn't matter. No, he had no children.

He lived with a woman, an old woman who looked after him. It was she who had told him that this enemy of his had set obeah on him. She was a sort of obeah-woman herself, but her obeah was not strong enough to offset the effect of the other's.

The old woman, Mag, was sick, and almost starved to death. But if Missis bought 'Black Magic' he would be able to fix all that. He would get doctor's medicine for her, he would be able to see a man about this man who had 'set duppy on him'. No, he wouldn't take money from her like that. He mustn't. If he had any money he would be sure to put it on 'Black Magic' and then the filly wouldn't win.

But if she bought 'Black Magic', if 'Black Magic' did win . . . If she made a lot of money off the filly, then perhaps she would always come to him for tips. He knew them all. If the man who had set obeah on him didn't find out about it, they could enter into a profitable business arrangement. But for God's sake she must tell no one.

'My dear, he was positively living up to his appearance. If he had tried he couldn't have been better – more creepy-queer and positively mysterious.'

A pleasing little shudder went through the company. A girl with a gentle, wistful face, who answered to the name of Margot, pulled her chair closer, and leaned over earnestly, expectantly.

'Perfectly priceless, eh Babs?' Jimmy Crone ejaculated.

'I believe Ruth is just having the time of her life at our expense,' said a tall youngster with a laugh. 'She's just making it up as she goes along.'

'Peter, don't be an ass,' a willowy blonde with a drawl, retorted. 'How could dear Ruth make up a story half so fascinating. That sort of thing requires imagination, and a flair of creating suspense, and all that, which is not Ruth's line at all. Now Margot – can't you see how Margot is simply drinking it up? We may yet read about it in the form of another of those delightfully realistic short stories of Margot's that she somehow gets into the local mags. Though why she does it I for one cannot tell.'

'Oh, Margot's a dear little socialist, darling, didn't you know?' This was answered by a general titter.

'Please go on, Ruth,' Margot said, quietly.

'Well just then he must have seen someone coming, for he gave his arm a wrench and slunk away. He was lost among the crowd before I could stop him. It was Lance Ruddock, my dear,' with a becoming glow. 'You know how Lance is. He simply made me tell him. And then, he laughed as though he would never stop. I was quite annoyed with him. And then he told me something about Joe Smith. He was an ex-jockey. He had been properly suspended for some dirty work on the race track. As a matter of fact it was principally due to Lance that he was exposed and suspended, and the man had had the nerve to accuse Lance – Lance Ruddock, of all people, who everybody knows is just rolling – of having bribed him.'

Ruth sipped her cocktail and set it down on the arm of her chair. Then she took up the threads of her story.

She saw the man for the last time just as she was leaving the race track. He slid up to her side out of nowhere, in the minute that Lance had left her for some reason or the other. In his eyes there was the shrewd, quick look of a caged mongoose. He stood looking at her expectantly. And then the most perfectly awful thing happened.

She had to tell him that she had not bought 'Black Magic' after all!

'Well, don't all look at me like that! After all Lance told me definitely not to trust the man, that he was just trying to get something out of me. Lance told me to buy ''Scorpion'', so I put my shirt on ''Scorpion''.'

There was a silence.

'Good God! I remember now. That was the day when Major Trumpet's filly ''Black Magic'' paid something like twelve pounds ten to win. I thought I did recognise the name, though no one had hardly heard of the horse before. Whew!'

'Well, I couldn't know that could I? Besides Lance . . . Oh, all right then – '

'Well, there is nothing more to tell, really. All I remember is that a horrible look came into his eyes. I have never seen such a horrible look in anyone's eyes before. I . . . I felt really sorry for him. It was a horrible haunted look . . . with something of horrible hunger about it too . . .'

She paused. Then suddenly she got up and started to giggle. 'He . . . he snatched my handbag then and ran. There was a kind of commotion. I am not at all sure I was aware of what was going on in me. I started laughing. I was laughing like hell when Lance came up and bundled me into the car before the police could start taking statements.'

Margot went up to her and put an arm around her, and someone handed her a cocktail which she swallowed at a single gulp.

'The . . . funniest part about it, though . . . you haven't heard that yet,' she laughed leaning against Margot. 'There wasn't a pen . . . penny in m-my purse! Lance told me to buy ''Scorpion'' . . . I . . . I put my shirt on ''Scorpion''.'

Blackout

THE city was in partial blackout, the street lights had not been turned on, on account of the wartime policy of conserving electricity, and the houses behind their discreet arelia hedges were wrapped in an atmosphere of exclusive respectability.

The young woman waiting at the bus stop was not in the least nervous, in spite of the wave of panic that had been sweeping the city about bands of hooligans roaming the streets after dark and assaulting unprotected women. She was a sensible young woman to begin with, who realized that one good scream would be sufficient to bring a score of respectable suburban householders running to her assistance. On the other hand she was an American, and fully conscious of the tradition of American young women that they don't scare easily.

Even that slinking blacker shadow that seemed to be slowly materialising out of the darkness at the other side of the street did not disconcert her. She was only slightly curious now that she observed that the shadow was approached her.

It was a young man dressed in conventional shirt and pants, with a pair of canvas shoes on his feet. That was what lent the suggestion of slinking to his movements, because he went along noiselessly; that, and the mere suggestion of a stoop. For he was very tall. And there was a curious look as of a great hunger or unrest about the eyes. But the thing that struck her immediately was the fact that he was black; the other particulars scarcely made any impression at all as against that. In her country it is not every night that a white woman would be likely to be thus nonchalantly approached by a black man. There was enough of novelty in all this to intrigue her. She seemed to remember that any sort of adventure could happen to you in one of these tropical islands of the West Indies.

'Could you give me a light, lady?' the man said.

True she was smoking, but she had only just lit this one from the stub of the cigarette she had thrown away. The fact was she had no matches. Would he believe her, she wondered.

'I am sorry, I haven't got a match.'

The young man looked into her face, seemed to hestitate an instant and said, his brow slightly in perplexity: 'But you are smoking.'

There was no argument against that. Still she was not particular about giving him a light from the cigarette she was smoking. It may be stupid, but there was a suggestion of intimacy about such an act, simple as it was, that, call it what you may, she just could not accept offhand.

There was a moment's hesitation on her part now, during which time the man's steady gaze never left her face. There was something of pride and challenge in his look, and curiously mingled with that, something of quiet amusement too.

She held out her cigarette toward him between two fingers.

'Here,' she said, 'you can light from that.'

In the act of bending his head to accept the proffered light, he had perforce to come quite close to her. He did not seem to understand that she meant him to take the lighted cigarette from her hand. He just bent over her hand to light his.

Presently he straightened up, inhaled a deep lungful of soothing smoke and exhaled again with satisfaction. She saw then that he was smoking the half of a cigarette, that had been clinched and saved for future consumption.

'Thank you,' said the man, politely; and was in the act of moving off when he noticed that instead of returning her cigarette to her lips she had casually, unthinkingly flicked it away. He observed all these things in the split part of a second that it took him to say those two words. It was almost a whole cigarette she had thrown away. She had been smoking it with evident enjoyment a moment before.

He stood there looking at her, with a sort of cold speculation.

In a way it unnerved her. Not that she was frightened. He seemed quite decent in his own way, and harmless; but he made her feel uncomfortable. If he had said something rude she would have preferred it. It would have been no more than she would have expected of him. But instead, this quiet contemptuous look. Yes, that was it. The thing began to take on definition in her mind. How dare he; the insolence!

'Well, what are you waiting for?' she said, because she felt she had to break the tension somehow.

'I am sorry I made you waste a whole cigarette,' he said.

She laughed a little nervously. 'It's nothing,' she said, feeling a fool.

'There's plenty more where that came from, eh?'

'I suppose so.'

This would not do. She had no intention of standing at a street corner jawing with – well, with a black man. There was something indecent about it. Why didn't he move on? As though he had read her thoughts he said.

'This is the street lady. It's public.'

Well, anyway she didn't have to answer him. She could snub him quietly, the way she should have properly done from the start.

'It's a good thing you're a woman,' he said.

'And if I were a man?'

'As man to man maybe I'd give you something to think about,' he said, still in that quiet even voice.

In America they lynched them for less than that, she thought.

'This isn't America,' he said. 'I can see you are an American. In this country there are only men and women. You'll learn about that if you stop here long enough.'

This was too much. But there was nothing she could do about it. But yes there was. She could humour him. Find out what his ideas were about this question, anyway. It would be something to talk about back home. Suddenly she was intrigued.

'So in this country there are only men and women, eh?'

'That's right. So to speak there is only you an' me, only there are hundreds of thousands of us. We seem to get along somehow without lynchings and burnings and all that.'

'Do you really think that all men are created equal?'

'It don't seem to me there is any sense in that. The facts show it ain't so. Look at you an' me, for instance. But that isn't to say you're not a woman the same way as I am a man. You see what I mean?'

'I can't say I do.'

'You will though, if you stop here long enough.'

She threw a quick glance in his direction.

The man laughed.

'I don't mean what you're thinking,' he said. 'You're not my type of woman. You don't have anything to fear under that heading.'

'Oh!'

'You're waiting for the bus, I take it. Well that's it coming now. Thanks for the light.'

'Don't mention it,' she said, with a nervous sort of giggle.

He made no attempt to move along as the bus came up. He stood there quietly aloof, as though in the consciousness of a male strength and pride that was just his. There was something about him that was at once challenging and disturbing. He had shaken her supreme confidence in some important sense.

As the bus moved off she was conscious of his eyes' quiet scrutiny of her, without the interruption of artificial barriers; in the sense of dispassionate appraisement, as between man and woman; any man, any woman.

She fought resolutely against the very natural desire to turn her head and take a last look at him. Perhaps she was thinking about what the people on the bus might think. And perhaps it was just as well that she did not see him bend forward with that swift hungry movement, retrieving from the gutter the half-smoked cigarette she had thrown away.

Lunch Hour Rush

THE vacant tables were filling up rapidly. The hum of conversation grew steadily in volume. A Ham-and-Eggs over by the window camouflaged himself behind a newspaper and watched the pageant of feminine legs crossing and recrossing the busy street below. He was a connoisseur of feminine pulchritude from the waist down. He was past middle age, bald on top, and a bachelor.

'Coffee or dessert?'

He raised his eyes to those of the little waitress who effervesced with latent energy.

'Coffee. Black.'

As Milly turned briskly to another table, his eyes raked her fore and aft. This girl was a knowing one. She never came near enough to enable him to pinch her under cover of the tablecloth. On one occasion he had asked her to turn the window so as to manoeuvre her between the table and the wall. She would have to come close then, because she was not tall enough to reach the window otherwise. He could place the newspaper carelessly in such a position as to cover the stealthy approach of his hand . . . but Milly had unexpectedly come all the way round the table, approaching the window from the other side. This little manoeuvre on her part had entirely upset all his carefully arranged plans. He had been outflanked, defeated. A smart little girl was Milly. He had tried to cover up his chagrin with a short laugh.

Milly was on her toes now. She was the smartest, most popular waitress in the place. She got the most tips, the biggest ones. But if she kept on like this she would have a nervous breakdown. In spite of her occasional dizzy-spells she had to keep on being as bright as a new sixpence, courteous, quick. She had always to keep her wits about her too.

She had her regular customers who waited for her to come and get their orders, and there were new customers dropping in all the while who kept crooking their fingers at her and trying to catch her eye.

The Usual, over by the left wing, was sometimes very trying. He was a vegetarian with a sour face and disposition, as though life disagreed with him. He complained about something or the other two out of three times. His tips, when they did come, were a couple of coppers at the most.

Then there were the two typists who although they worked in different buildings, always met at lunch time, generally at their own special table. One would not order until the other arrived. The moment they got together they acted as though they were old school friends who had not met in years and were overwhelmed with joy at this chance encounter, they had so much to tell each other, they talked so excitedly with so many 'my dear's' and giggles. One could hardly wait for the other to finish a sentence. It seemed too they did not care who overheard what they said, so that by the odd bits of sentences let fall in her presence, Milly, if she had had the desire, could have reconstructed the biographies of those two city typists with scarcely an effort.

'. . . my dear, I am certain he said Colon – not Columbia. He'll be taking the plane, of course, and he has promised to write me everyday by air-mail. Do you think my organdie would look well trimmed with green?'

'How are you making it? I saw Elsie with something terrific with green taffeta trimmings. And that reminds me about "Bold Aventure" . . . I don't mean the racehorse . . .'

A transient Hamburger Steak caught Milly's eye and crooked a beckoning finger in her direction. Milly answered his flattering eyes with a non-committal smile. Milly thought: 'I am going to ask him for the last time this evening, just as he is through checking the cash. I'm going to put it squarely to him – no nonsense . . . and if he tries to get fresh with me again I'll slap his face this time, job or no job. And if he says "No," I'm going to ask for two weeks leave to go to the country. If I get it, it will be without pay, but I need the rest, and Phil and I can do some close figuring in those two weeks . . .'

The Hamburger Steak gave her a shilling extra.

'For yourself,' he said, and held her hand for an instant as she took the money from him.

Milly smiled her most non-committal smile. 'Thank you.'

'Doing anything tonight?'

'Nothing special. But I expect the boyfriend will be around as usual. We may go to a show, or just sit on our own bit of porch and hold hands.'

She paused for an instant at the table of the Usual, and noted the mess of herbs seemed to please him for once. He even spared her a sort of smile, embellished with a quivering lettuce leaf.

One of her late customers was coming in. He was early today. He wore his usual absent-minded air, but Milly could tell that something unusual had happened. Something exciting. His smile was a little less impersonal, his eyes didn't look quite so tired . . .

'Congratulations,' said Milly.

He warmed to her immediately. His smile was really attractive now. It subtly deprived his face of years of accumulated lines, making him seem younger, more full of beans.

'Thank you, Milly. It took a long time coming, but you know, now that it has happened it makes one feel it was well worth waiting for.'

She didn't know what in the world he was talking about, of course, what it was that had happened, but what difference did it make!

It was not until she returned with the soup that he realized this girl couldn't possibly know the nature of his good-fortune. He asked her point-blank: 'Why did you congratulate me just now?'

She answered him with a smile – the one she reserved for her friends.

'Oh I don't know. I just saw you looking happy, that's all. Does it matter?'

He laughed outright, taking a small memo-book from his pocket.

'Do you mind if I make a note of this? You see, I'm a writer. I have just had my first book accepted.'

She said: 'How splendid!' Then after a pause: 'Here's something else you might put in your book. I once said the same thing to a man simply because he was wearing a new suit of clothes – you know, cut differently, and all that. It gave him a new personality. He positively blushed, and looked self-conscious when he tried to smile. I learnt after that he had just lost his wife!'

She went away before he had had time to fully digest the point of her little story.

'. . . my dear, he said the most delicious thing to me, and would you believe it, he danced the next *three* numbers in succession with her! I made Jerry take me to the bar just to see what was going on between them, and there they were together as thick as thieves. She's a brassy little bitch, that's what!' To Milly: 'Have you got Cherry Sundae on the menu today? Or shall we share a Banana Split? I couldn't go a whole one of those things myself. You know, I weighed last Tuesday, and was positively horrified to find I had put on three pounds, and it's all around the waistline. Very well then, make it two small Cherry Sundaes. Everytime I think of Cherry Sundae I remember Dickie . . . Don't you remember Dickie . . . the time with Gerald, out at Palm Beach? The same time when Muriel filled her shoe with sand and poured it down his back. Did I ever tell you what happened afterwards between Muriel and the Dennis boy? I got it from Gladys – no, not Boysie's Gladys – who used to be friendly with Bertie Simmonds while his wife was away in the country . . .'

Ham-and-Eggs was dawdling over his black coffee. He crooked a finger in Milly's direction, but she feigned not to see him. She was hurrying to take the orders of five young lawyers who always occupied a large table in the centre. If their table was taken before they arrived, they would push two smaller ones together. They talked and laughed loud enough to be heard by the lunchers around them. Their jokes were not exactly 'drawing-room', and their sublest wit usually had to do with sexy matters – but they didn't try to date her or pinch her. They didn't address their remarks to her directly, though they were not above speaking *at* her, obliquely, their real meaning thinly veiled beneath a veneer of what passed in their particular circle for wit. They were not really altogether vicious – most of them.

It hurt, rather than annoyed her. Somehow she felt sorry for these jaded, unhappy young men. She smiled mechanically in response to their indirect sallies, took their orders mechanically too, as though she were thinking about something else.

She was too, she was thinking about Phil, and what she was going to say to the boss that very evening. Either he would give her that raise of pay, or she would try to find another job. She wasn't going to stand any nonsense from him, either. Phil was becoming impatient. His manner of late was irritable and his moods unpredictable. He wanted to get married On his salary alone they could not afford it. But he was all for her leaving the restaurant and taking a shot at it. She was businesslike, though, and careful. They must save a substantial nest-egg first. She could save next to nothing on her present pay.

Either he would give her that long promised raise, or she would ask for two weeks leave. She could get a doctor's certificate to show that she needed the rest . . . those dizzy-spells . . . she was tired, she needed those two weeks anyway.

A friend of hers had found lucrative work in a beauty parlour. There were other things a girl with her looks and abilities could do, other jobs she could get. Although she had never done any other job or work than waiting in a restaurant, she had a high school education and had been training for teaching. She had taken this job because, staying in the city with relatives none too well off, just after leaving college, the necessity of securing employment had become increasingly imperative. She had had to forgo her ambitions, for the time being, she told herself, and take the first job that presented itself. Ever after that she had been too busy, or too tired to think about anything else.

And then she met Phil. Phil was a mechanic. He worked at a garage where the hours were long and the pay small, quite insufficient to keep them both. When he asked for a raise of pay the management spoke darkly of certain impending reductions to the staff on the grounds of retrenchment, which never materialised. If they could save enough money for Phil to open a shop, now, things would be different. It was their only hope as far as she could see . . . unless they could find somebody willing to put up the capital . . .'

' . . . I just had to put him in his place, my dear. I told him off properly. Made him understand that he was not my boss. I have had occasion to report him to the boss twice before. He'd better watch his step, he's got a wife and two children, and I reminded him. That's three good reasons why he should want to hang on to his job with his teeth, instead of trying to order me about and tell me what I ought to do. "Miss Ainsworth," he says through his false teeth, which never seem to be quite secure in his mouth, "these returns will have to be typed over." "Typed over by who?" I asked him, just like that. He gets very red in the face like a turkey-cock. "I couldn't think of sending them to Head Office like that," he says, throwing them at me. "Don't know what New York would think we were paying typists' salaries for," he says, while I just went on powdering my nose, ignoring him. "If I pass returns like that," he says, getting redder and redder, "I'll soon be out of a job." I started laughing then and that made him all the madder. "You'll be out of a job quicker if you don't learn to behave like a gentleman." I said, and he gave *such* a look; I nearly *died* laughing.'

Milly turned away from the table and started down the passage with a tray of empties. Suddenly, unaccountably she felt light-headed, as though she would like to giggle, for no particular reason. And again that spasm of dizziness . . . She thought: Supposing everything should start going round and round the way it sometimes did when she had these spells badly – and she should fall with that tray of plates and dishes right in the middle of this place full of people! Wouldn't that be funny? She leaned against a concrete column for a moment; not so much because of the giddiness, as in order to enable her to get control over that terrible desire to laugh outright and to send the tray spinning away from her with a clatter to the tiled floor . . . or right in the lap of Ham-and-Eggs over yonder. With a well directed putt she could manage it . . . her arm gave a little involuntary twitch at the shoulder . . . and then through the corner of her eye she saw Phil come in. She held her breath slowly, and took her lower lip between her teeth.

Phil's face looked odd. Something had happened to him. She had never seen him look like this before. She swallowed hard . . . Phil needed someone to take care of him. He wasn't even eating properly these days, not enough to keep an infant going . . . She would put it to him squarely this very evening. It didn't matter now if he should fire her then and there. Phil came first – he needed her. She would say 'yes' and they could get married at the Registry as soon as he wanted. She would get another job – a better one she was sure. Either he raised her pay, or . . .

Walking firmly now, brave in the strength of her new resolve, she went across to Phil to take his order. He didn't look up. It was as though he was afraid to meet her eyes.

'Order, sir?' she said, playfully.

'Hell, Milly . . .!' He turned a haggard face to her, and looked away again.

Her own face suddenly blanched. Before he said it she had guessed.

'What is it, Phil? You can tell me the worst,' she said, calmly. 'Together we can take it, no matter how bad . . .'

Her hand trembled with the desire to touch his unruly hair, there was a physical tightening of her breasts to have his face crushed against them.

'Well, it's just as bad as you think.'

'You mean . . .?'

'Yes, they gave me the boot. Same old story – retrenching!'

She passed a weary hand across her forehead, pushing back a stray strand of hair that flirted about her cheek.

Two tables away the Usual was cocking an imperative finger at her. He wanted his bill.

'Be back in a minute,' she said, laying a hand on his arm.

'That spinach was damn rotten,' said the Usual, grimly.

'Did you enjoy the vegetable salad, sir?' mechanically.

'Br-r-r-rh!'

She was glad to get away to the next customer who awaited her. So Phil had lost his job. Funny that she had never considered that possibility, had not therefore been able to shape her plans against such a contingency. She'd have to revise all her ideas now, of course.

She couldn't go to the boss with her ultimatum as she had planned. That was out. She'd have to hang on to this job with her teeth now. Till something turned up . . .

Ham-and-Egg's leering face just didn't register on her consciousness now. She went up to the table like one who moved in a trance, and started loading her tray with empty plates, dishes. He took a generous portion of her flesh between his finger and thumb under cover of the newspaper . . .

'Don't do that!' she said, sharply. She looked at him as though she would like to dump the tray with its load of dishes right on top of his bald head. For a moment only, the look she gave him was frightening in its ferocity. The next moment she had recovered control of herself. She was smiling at him, even. The first and last rule of the restaurant was that you must be civil to the customers.

She said, coyly: 'You shouldn't do that, sir. It makes me black-and-blue there. Then I won't be able to wear my new bathing suit to the beach Sunday morning, the boyfriend isn't colour-blind, you know . . .'

Had to be civil to the customers. What did it matter to the management if a girl's bottom was pinched once in a while?

He laughed and tipped her generously. She looked at him coquettishly . . . made round-eyes at him . . .

'H-m-m-m! If that's what a gal gets for being pinched . . .!'

Yes, she had a way with men. Of course, that was what made her of value to the boss. She was the best waitress in the place. Pretty, capable, quick, uncomplaining . . . and she'd got a way with the male customers.

Again that horrible dizziness . . . She really needed the vacation badly, but she would not dare to ask for it now. Too risky.

Balancing the tray she walked easily, gracefully between the tables . . . she lurched against one of them, the one where five young men sat. Somebody laughed. She tried to steady herself with a hand on the back of a chair. Everybody seemed to be staring at her, wondering if she were drunk. Somebody said: 'Hi, Milly . . .!' and something else – she didn't hear the last part of the sentence. The chairs and tables were going round and round in a whirl. This would not do, she must get a grip of herself . . . Somebody laughed . . . The chairs and tables did a wild dance before her eyes . . . she was falling, falling . . .

The crash of the plates and dishes clattering against the tiled floor created quite a stir among the lunchers. It brought the boss himself from his office.

'Take her in my room,' he said generously, to Phil and the man who called himself a writer, as they lifted her up from the floor. He held the swing-door of his private office open for them himself. There was a couch inside. They laid her upon the couch, and somebody telephoned for a doctor.

'What she needs is rest,' the boss confided to Phil, in the tone of one who knows about these things, 'a good long rest. Luckily I had a likely looking girl from the country in here this very morning looking for a job – pretty too. I have her name and address down on my memo-pad somewhere. I must get in touch with her right away . . . When she gets well again, maybe . . . we'll see what we can do for her anyway . . .'

'Now where the hell did I put that memo-pad?'

World's End

It was a cheerless morning, the sky was overcast with grey opaque vapour like a veil. Every third person or so that you passed in the street coughed, and each one seemed as dispirited as the next. You saw the sadness of people now, even under the casual laughter and the bravado of indifference.

Old Ben walked along without looking to the right or left of him, and the boy pattered along behind. The old man had forgotten that they had not had any breakfast, and that he was hungry. He walked with the sort of aimless desperation of a man who has nowhere to go; but it seemed to him necessary, although barren of result.

The boy, uncomplaining, walking always a little behind, reminded Old Ben of his presence by suddenly giving way to a fit of coughing, precipitated by that tickling burning feeling in his throat. Ben stopped, suddenly remembered the boy, breakfast; remembered that Tim must be hungry; thinking suddenly of hunger, emptiness, his own loss, and his emptiness in a world of emptiness; passing from one bleak facade to the next, a shop.

They went inside, and Ben bought a threepenny loaf of bread, paid threepence more and the Chinaman obligingly cut the loaf right in two down the middle lengthwise and smeared butter on both sides facing, clamped them together shut, and Ben taking it broke the loaf in two passed one portion to the boy.

They ate breaking pieces out of the loaf with finger and thumb, chewing solidly with steady unbroken rhythm of facial muscles, like men who are at the business of eating, the utterly simplified motions of necessity, eating; without waste of energy, without loss of motion, getting the business done.

They left the shop, walking the streets again, eating their breakfast as they went.

Sudden lighting sun breaking now, putting their shadows behind them. Coming out of the mist of vapour like veil, welcome, another and necessary. No loss here, either, no waste of motion. They quickened their pace, as though an urgency compelled; another necessity thrust upon them, to suit their pace to the sun.

The next place of call going the round of his regular customers, the yard in which three separate families lived. He knocked on the gate. A young woman came out, not recognising him; a man too, walking toward him coming from the back of the premises.

'Why, it is Mass Ben! How-do, Mass Ben. Where you' cart is,' said the woman.

'Ah, me daughter.'

'I didn't know it was who. What happen?'

'Nothing today? What become of you' cart?' said the man.

Both of them saying the same things, asking the same questions; always the same. They did not recognise him, either. He passed it on with the barest lift of his shoulders.

'Donkey died las' night. Got bellyache. Jus' lay down an' died.'

'You mean it!' The man made a sound with his tongue against his teeth. The woman said nothing, to her scarcely something of matter, the death of a donkey. So it had been everywhere he went, calling at each house on a barren and useless mission, but to him necessary.

At each house he had recited the same thing. His donkey had died in the night. No more cart, no more yams potatoes cabbages red peas cho-cho for sale, or anything; no more business, nothing to do. Nothing to live by from day to day, buying and selling his goods. And he thought it unquestionable and necessary that they should know. And the same questions asked always, and the same answers.

'What you going to do now?'

He hadn't had time to think about that. It was odd that they should all think of the same things to say; or was it? He hadn't had time to give that matter a thought. They spoke about it sympathetically, jokingly, like the man and the woman here.

'You could sell the skin. They give you ten shillings for it at the tannery, I hear say,' said the man.

'Ten shillings,' said Ben, saying the words over in his mouth, but without meaning. What did ten shillings have to do with the matter, where was the connection. He was talking about something else, surely.

'Ten shillings is not to be sneezed at,' said the man.

Of course not, was anybody saying it wasn't so! But there was always this fact, and that was another, and there was no slightest connection between the two.

He looked stupid, standing there, blinking at them in the sun. The boy stood a little apart, looking on, as though he wasn't involved.

'When is the funeral?' said the woman, and laughed. Looking at his stupid old face she couldn't help laughing. He was funny.

'Funeral?' said Old Ben.

And when he said that you couldn't help feeling what a stupid old man he was. The woman laughed again, and went inside.

They left that house and went on to the next, and the rest of them in this street, and then they left this street and went on to the next, and so on, walking useless miles.

About noon the sun came out bright. The day cleared. The boy came abreast of the old man catching his attention by tugging at his sleeve.

'Papa, let us go home now,' he said.

'You tired, boy?'

'No. But let us go home all the same.'

'But how can we. We still have places to go; wait; I know what. You must be hungry again, we will stop and eat.'

'I am not hungry,' the boy said.

But he couldn't explain anything more to the old man. When the people laughed he felt a curious sense of shame, although he always stood aloof from it as though he were not involved. He too looking at that helpless, stupid old face blinking in the sun, felt it; but he didn't laugh. It came as a raw revelation; he had never thought of his papa in this way before – seeing him so now, he was ashamed for his father and for himself. He was conscious always of the others' laughter, and his own shame.

He tried again to persuade the old man.

'Let us go home now, Papa,' he begged, but old Ben either would not or could not bring his mind to this; there was always only that other.

'We will get another donkey,' the boy wheedled as an older person might try to coax a petulant child. 'We will get us another donkey, Papa,' tugging at his sleeve to bring his attention back to him.

They went into a shop and the old man bought a threepenny loaf of bread and a small parcel of brown sugar. He borrowed a quart measure from the buxom woman who served in the shop, and drew water from a tap in the yard. He put the sugar in the water and stirred it, and with this beverage they washed down the bread.

After they had eaten they sat on the shop piazza and rested. The old man leaned back against the wall and closed his eyes. The boy sat upright, alert, watching the old man.

A fly settled on his nose, and he came awake suddenly. He rubbed the back of his hand against his nose and sat up. It was raining now, he saw. He hadn't known when it had started to rain, so he must have been asleep. The boy was sitting across from him, his face was screwed up, crying.

'What's this,' said the old man. 'What you crying for?'

'Nothing,' said the boy.

'You cry for nothing, then,' said the old man. 'What sense to cry for nothing, boy?'

The boy sniffed loudly, without shame. Some people sheltering on the shop piazza from the rain looked down incuriously at the old man and the boy.

The old man said in a gruff voice: 'Here, son,' fumbling in his pocket the while. He said: 'I wouldn't have brought you out at all if I knew you was goin' to carry on in this way.'

The boy sat dejectedly rubbing his eyes.

'Here you want a penny?'

'No,' said the boy.

'What you want, then?'

'I want to go home.'

'Well, bless me,' said the old man. 'I thought you was crying for something.'

Then he started to upbraid the boy, calling him names, saying he was no son of his, to make a spectacle of himself like that before people.

'They are laughing at you,' said the old man. 'Shut it up this minute, you hear, before I clout you on the head.'

Presently the boy stopped crying.

'Here's a penny,' the old man said.

The boy took the coin and put it in his pocket.

'Well, bless me,' said the old man.

The boy coughed; and the old man grumbled under his breath about people catching their death of cold walking in the rain.

'Can't go home until it stops raining,' said the old man querulously.

As though it was a cue for which he was unconsciously waiting, the boy started coughing again. He coughed and coughed.

The rain beat down on the zinc roof in a steady downpour that drowned out every other sound.

'See what you would have caught? Must be want your death of cold,' the old man grumbled.

The sun came out and it stopped raining. And the people who were sheltering on the shop piazza moved along – all except the old man and the boy. People came and went, a trickle of people passing all the time, but still the old man and the boy sat on.

Presently the old man went inside the shop. The boy remained outside with curious aloofness, his hands thrust in his pockets, looking out into the street.

As twilight closed in the street seemed to shrink, to become narrower, as though the sidewalks had drawn closer.

Inside the shop the old man was explaining to the woman behind the counter about the loss of the donkey, the loss of his business, and the fact that there was no money, and the woman listened without laughing. Nor did she try to tell him that the skin would fetch him ten shillings at the tannery. She just listened while the old man talked and talked, with awareness in her intelligent eyes.

Outside on the piazza the boy stood listlessly watching the dusk closing in on the street, and the people coming and going, and sometimes stopping to greet each other passing the good of the day. A dray drove furiously down the street and people gave way on either side, so that the yelling drayman flourishing and cracking his whip seemed like a charioteer driving through the opposing ranks of an enemy horde.

The stars came out one by one and filled the sky.

Inside the shop the old man babbled on, reciting the inexhaustible tale of his loss – like a man relating the story of it, who had witnessed the end of the world.

Ten years ago, he said, he had buried his wife. She had been a good woman, and they had had three sons. They had buried one while he was still at the breast; the last. Seven years after his eldest son, the apple of his eye, had died, leaving only the boy, that was Tim. Tim was all he had left. There was now only himself and Tim. All his life he seemed to have accumulated nothing but losses, there was no money, nothing to show for it all. Last evening he had stabled the donkey, he said, and before dusk it had laid down with the bellyache and died. It was a good donkey, he said, gentle and amiable as a lamb. He had had it seven years.

Part III

Some Women Take a Whipping

WHEN they brought the news to Sadie Blum how Maxie had got killed outright in a boiler explosion at the packing plant where he worked, everybody wondered about the way she took it.

To start with she didn't cry. Her face sort of froze over hard and she put the back of her hand up to wipe a stray wisp of hair out of her eyes, passing it across her forehead with the gesture of a tired child.

The only thing she said was: 'Did he die – right away? Or did he hang on for a time?'

'He must have died in an instant, because he was right up against it when it burst,' Mack told her, because he was the leader of the little deputation that had been appointed by Maxie's co-workers to break the news to his young widow.

'Was better so,' said Mack, turning his hat around in his hand.

The others had put theirs down when they came into the tiny living room, but he held on to his as though he was afraid to let it go.

'Yeah. I guess it was better so,' said Tiny in his hoarse bass voice.

'Seein' he had to go that way,' said Mack.

And Jerry, the foreman of their shift said: 'I reckon it was.'

Then the three of them looked at her, sitting there with her hands folded on her lap, as though they were waiting for something, as though there was something wanting about the whole show. They sat there, shifting about uneasily, like bum actors waiting for their cue.

'Well, I guess that's all,' said Mack, getting to his feet at length. He held his hat in both hands in front of him and stood looking down at his boots, and shifted his weight from one foot to the other. And then as though conscious of the need for variety he lifted one foot and rubbed it up and down the underside of the other leg.

The other men got up too and came and stood beside Mack before the little woman for a while, and then they said goodbye, they had to go.

And all the while she sat there, saying nothing, doll-like and flower-like and like nothing they had ever seen in a woman before.

That evening at supper Mack spoke little, thinking about Maxie, who had always been popular with everyone. And thinking about Maxie's widow. And then suddenly he said:

'Dang it, Mary, I just can't figure it out no how,' shaking his head, and drawing crosses with the handle of his fork on the table cloth.

'I know,' said Mary McIntosh. 'I know just how you feel, Mack. It must be a horrible way to go.'

'It's not that,' said Mack. And she looked at him.

'It's not that I'm thinking about,' he said. 'It's the way his wife took it, when we went to break the bad news.'

'Oh?'

'Yes. She just sat there like that, like – like something out of this world. And not even a tear.'

'Poor girl.'

'She didn't even *say* anything. Beats me. Don't seem natural like. I guess some women take a whipping to make 'em cry.'

And Mary said it must have been on account of it coming to her as such a shock – him alive and laughing and chucking the youngster in the air and catching him again and kissing Sadie goodbye at the door, and then . . .

That very evening Mary put on her street clothes after she had washed up the supper dishes and went to call on Sadie.

She found the little woman in the bedroom sitting beside the baby's cot, and she noticed that Sadie was finishing the knitting she had been doing on a man's sweater, and that more than anything else gave her a turn.

So she sat down on the bed beside the younger woman, and put an arm about her and said:

'My dear. My poor dear girl.'

She said: 'What you want is a good hearty cry.'

But Sadie didn't cry. She rose and put away her knitting, folding it neatly with the red and green plastic needles tucked safely away inside. And she put it away carefully in the very bottom of the middle bureau drawer, and pushed the drawer shut with her knees.

Mary watched her closely, noting every single action, as though she was storing them away for future reference.

Sadie came back and sat down on the bed, and the baby was asleep in its crib which had been drawn up close to the bed. And it too seemed to Mary McIntosh like something doll-like and flower-like and altogether out of the world, lying there with one fist tightly shut upon nothing on the pillow beside its head, and with a half-smile on its lips that showed the glistening tip of a single tooth.

Mary said: 'There, there you let it go. Just put your head down, dearie, and let it go.'

And then a deep and wonderful sympathy, such as is given only to some women, welled up in her, and she put her head down on Sadie's shoulder and started to weep.

Presently she lifted her head, her face disfigured and obliterated with tears, and went across to the bureau and put on her hat, careful to see that it sat on her head just right. And then she came back and kissed Sadie on both cheeks and said: 'You'll surely feel better now, dearie,' and went out leaving the girl sitting there.

Sadie sat on like that for a long time, her hands folded on her lap in that same defenceless attitude, looking down at the baby in its cot, her attention focused upon the pearly tip that was all that showed of its single tooth.

And the shadows came in from the window and multiplied themselves upon the floor.

And as it got darker inside the room a spot of soft light glowed more and more intensely where Maxie only yesterday had put luminous paint all over the switch beside the door, so that coming in he could find it easily in the dark. He had rigged it so that that switch operated a shaded night-light that wouldn't awaken her or the baby if he should come in late.

Presently she rose and went across to the window and put the curtains aside. They were the new curtains she had finished only the day before. She had put them up that morning thinking to herself what Maxie would say when he came home and saw them. Because Maxie was the kind of man who noticed such things. All sorts of little things.

If she brushed her hair away from one side of her face, instead of bringing it out full all round in the usual way, he'd notice that. He would take notice if she looked tired when he came home from work one evening. He noticed it the first time she put out the little book ends of inlaid wood she had picked up cheap at a bargain sale. And once he went out and bought her a corsage of red carnations because it just matched the dress she was wearing, although they weren't going out anywhere.

She gazed out of the darkened window and could just barely see the dim uneven skyline atop of all those irregular buildings out there. And a trick of light made her see a dark figure dancing grotesquely on top of a chimney pot, but leaning all awry.

She turned away from the window now and went and lay down on the bed her face in the pillow, and her body went stiff all over like a piece of board. And she put her hand out and felt along the empty side of the bed until it came up blind against the other pillow and she drew it to her and held it hard against her side.

And for a second or two she shook and trembled all over like a leaf. And then she went all stiff again like a piece of hard board.

The baby on its cot came awake slowly out of a happy dream.

It had gone to sleep with its attention shut hard on the shiny circle of glowing light just beside the door.

It lay on its back now and kicked its plump little legs straight out. And when it got tired of doing that it took one foot in both hands and brought it right up to its mouth.

Then it chuckled and kicked its legs out straight again and made rapid passes in front of its face with its chubby fists. And then it made a baby-sound catching sight again of the softly glowing circle of luminance just beside the door.

The girl got up from the bed presently and her face was white and set and hard. And there was a hard glassy look in her eyes too. She stared down at the baby in its cot, and still nothing of all that softened there.

She passed the back of her hand across her forehead again, as though she was putting invisible wisps of hair out of her face. Then she went over to the bureau and began pulling open drawers.

She took out some baby clothes and set them out on the floor. Then she took out some of her own clothes and did the same. Some things she set out and others she put back. And then she took out a programme and a letter, and set them, with an old toothbrush that had been used for whitening shoes, and a handful of nickels in the toe of an old sock, on a half-sheet of newspaper, and did them up solemnly into a neat parcel.

When she had that lot all tied up carefully, she as carefully tied it again. Then she put back the programme and the old toothbrush inside the drawer and was going to put back the odd sock with the nickels too, but it was as though something arrested her hand halfway, and she shook the nickels out on to the floor.

She held the sock up in her hand and turned it over, and looked at it this way and that with a kind of puzzled frown on her face.

And then she pushed one hand down the sock and two of her fingers came out through a hole in the heel. And she held it up like that in front of her face and started to laugh. And she laughed and laughed, twisting herself to and fro in convulsions on the floor.

The baby commenced to cry in its cot. But she didn't hear it. It cried louder and louder, but still she didn't hear it. The sound of her own laughter filled her ears.

And then as abruptly she stopped laughing. And she brought the hand that was dressed up in the old sock close to her eyes, and suddenly pressed it hard against her face.

The baby had gone back to the old game of sucking its toe again, as though there was more comfort in that than in tears.

And presently there was no sound in the room at all, saving only the hard, fierce sobbing of the woman on the floor.

Listen, the Wind...

THE BANGING of the shutter had kept her awake all night. It was a hinged jalousie, and the lower hinge was broken. The wind took it and rattled it and let it go . . . until she was on the point of dropping off to sleep again, then it would shake it and bang it with tremendous thuds against her half-consciousness, until she wanted to get up and scream.

Joel's form stretched out beside her with an abandon of limbs that sprawled heavily and only occasionally twitched with little starts and prods against her side, filled her with a sort of dull resentment . . . that the slamming shutter that wrung tortures out of her should leave him so peaceful, so blissfully undisturbed.

Joel's gentle snoring was another prod against her peace of mind . . . that he could be so full of slumber, so unconscious of her burden of sleeplessness.

Tomorrow he would mend the broken shutter . . . always it was tomorrow . . . She smiled deeply – down inside herself. Joel's face bloated and sagging with the relaxation of total sleep, tugged at the involuntary strings of her sense of humour . . . made her aware of him as part of that self she had found in the wonderful merging of their two selves . . . as though she had given birth to that new, rapturous idea of Joel with the smooth, bloated cheeks of a boy – like the one you see sometimes on Valentine cards, with such ridiculously inadequate wings, and a ridiculous little bow and arrow.

The round, jolly impudence of that face sharing her pillow, as he always did while hugging his in a close embrace, she found urgent of her uttermost compassion, sympathy, understanding. That was why Joel, pretending to be smart and full of worldly wisdom, and full of big ideas of things he was always on the verge of pulling off that would bring the stars down about their feet and set them up for life in the midst of a heaven of fulfilment, never really cheated her of her simple, yet sublime understanding of Joel – an understanding that was more than half of pure adoration.

I was at times like this, when she came into a kingdom of her own, peopled with herself and Joel, and intimate with the little imps of laughter that shook within her, that she could smile deep down within herself . . . a woman with a secret . . . an enigma to the neighbours, because in spite of all their unkind gossip and forebodings of evil, she still kept her secret, and it defeated them, thwarted them, so that their tongues were robbed of that spell of evil that drips with slander and gossiping – like a scorpion that has been deprived of its sting.

The banging of the shutter jerked her out of unconsciousness, just as she was dropping off again . . .

All night long she lay awake and listened to the gossip of the wind. Strange how tonight the wind was full of foreboding . . . like the tongues of those gossiping old women – only worse, much worse, for the words that told of the evil to come were her own words, shaped in her own consciousness.

She turned over on her side and tried not to listen to the things that the wind about the trees outside, the wind against the banging shutter, was telegraphing to her waking brain.

Tomorrow was wash day. She would take the large round bath pan full of washing down to the river, where all the women of the village would be. Above the noise of the paddles with which they beat the clothes, with the soap in them, against smooth, round boulders to get the deep dirt out of them, would be heard the tongues of the women . . . the cruel tongues that tore secrets from the innermost recesses of homes and spread them out before the world like washing was spread upon the river bank . . . the idle tongues, never for a moment quiet, that slavered over another's wounds with gloating and laughter.

But her secret would be locked tight within her breast, and she would smile deep down inside herself. That smile would be etched upon the corners of her mouth, but that would only be the reflection of the other, just as the white shifts of the women shone up at the men passing over the bridge above, from the placid surface of the pool.

The hearty cries of the younger women and girls who had waded higher upstream to bathe naked under the shadows of some trees, reached her in occasional gusts. Once there was a wild scattering of shrill laughter, and little shrieks of terror that were without sincerity, as some young men, for the mischief of it, sauntered down to the pool where they knew the girls were bathing.

There was a bold exchange of challenges, retorts, spiced with elemental, good-natured teasing, that would have sounded coarse to the ears of their more sophisticated sisters. But these black girls were of an innocence and *naïveté* that defied the conventions of what was regarded as the license that might be allowed between men and women. The nakedness of their bodies under the frankly covetous stares of the men, left them not one scrap ashamed. Their hiding behind boulders and frantic splashing of water to form a curtain around them, was not because they were ashamed to be caught thus, without their clothes on, but in reproof of those impudent young men who would reveal the secrets of their body's loveliness.

She had left Joel at home busy working out the details of his latest scheme to get his hands on to a lump of cash, so he could go into business like his uncle who was making a fortune out of buying produce from all settlers and selling it to the big merchants in the city, and more recently had even been exporting it himself.

He had armed himself with hammer and nails with the intention of mending the broken shutter. He was all contrition in the morning when she told him of her sleepless night.

He found the ladder in the fowl house . . . the fowls had been using it as a roost. It too needed mending. As she was going out with the pan of washing on her head, he had just looked up from the ladder, his mouth full of nails, and waggled the hammer at her.

A gaunt old woman, with the stringy, pimpled neck, and sharp face of a crow, was saying in her cracked voice, that had an edge to it that reminded one of a saw: 'He'll break your heart, my fine hussy. You take my word for it. He'll spoil your sweet face for you, and that smile too.'

A stout woman laughed. Her strong arms were bare to the elbows, and she was wielding a paddle with savage grunts that seemed to indicate the satisfaction she got out of pounding at something – anything.

'That Joel of yours needs a strong woman to make a man out of him – to make him do something besides fritter away his time with women and dice. None of your milk-and-water kind for him, honey. After the first flavour wears off, he'll be sorry he ever tied himself to you . . . because you're the sort of weak creature that will never do no good to him. When he was foolin' round my Estelle – now there was a gal would have been a match for him – I told him straight he'd have to get himself a real job first, or else work the land his father left him. That sent him on his way. Then he took up with you.'

She plied her paddle with powerful strokes, as though driving home her words.

It was getting dusk when she left the river with her burden of clean linen heaped up in a white bundle that flowed over the rim of the pan. She walked with the grace of a goddess, balancing her load upon her head with a perfect sense of rhythm, going up even the steepest incline.

She had to hurry home in order to prepare supper in time.

They were vultures all of them . . . great flapping black vultures circling above the still living flesh upon which they hoped to feast.

The sound of an axe met her as she was coming through the gate. Somehow that sound cheered her. It was Joel splitting firewood to cook their supper. The steady rhythm of the axe contrasted comfortingly with the quick feminine staccato thwacks of the women's paddles that still echoed about her ears. It was a homely, agreeable sound. The slow smooth rhythm of it slowed about her, filling her breast. She smiled deep down inside her, taking out her secret as she did in quiet moments of revealment like these, to look at it with wonder, and a sort of gentle longing.

She sought to reconcile all things with the quotient of that . . . the fixed and constant idea of him that she held in her mind's ideal imaging . . . that rapturous idea of *her* Joel that she kept locked away in the secret place of her heart . . . the revelation of him that looked up at her and made demands upon all her woman's store of compassion and faith and understanding . . . how could she make these things known to those soulless harpies who would rob her of her happiness, of the barren satisfaction of knowing that she too had succumbed to the loss and canker of uninspired living. She cooked rice cakes and dumplings and set them before him with a hash made from what was left of Sunday's meat.

He ate ravenously without saying much. He was thoughtful and subdued this evening, as though he had something on his mind. She recognised the mood. It meant that he was being driven by his thoughts into channels of exploration down which the simple mind could not follow him. When he tried to explain his plans to her, her inability to keep pace with his nimble thinking, irritated him. She had learnt, when he had moods like these, not to ply him with questions. She thought, with that secret smile of hers, that those other women would have construed it differently. Their suspicious minds would instantly have accused him of infidelity. They would say 'He's got some mischief on his mind. Ten chances to one it's another woman he's thinking about.' But she knew differently.

He said, suddenly pushing his plate away from him: 'Why the hell don't you say something, instead of just standing there, staring at me like an idiot all the time? God, I didn't know I was marrying a dummy, a woman without any mind of her own!'

He pushed the chair away from under him so savagely that it was overturned, and strode past her through the door. She felt as though he had struck her.

Numbed, unthinking, she started mechanically to clear the dishes from the table.

Hours later, as she lay awake in bed, the portentous stillness of night suffocatingly thrown about her, shutting her off from those emotions that moved deeply within her, like currents of tide and wind moving across the face of the deep, she heard him coming up the path, singing light-heartedly, as though he had not a care in the world.

She heard him stop just outside the door of their bedroom and remove his boots. He came into the room in his bare feet, so as not to awaken her. She felt his breath on her cheek as he bent over to kiss her long and tenderly.

She longed with all her heart to take his head upon her breast then, to tell him that all was right and as it should be between them . . . that she would not have had anything of all that changed.

She was surprised that he should have been able to fall asleep so soon, so soundly, leaving her, a little shaken, a little bewildered, with a feeling of unfulfilment, on the brink of this new and wounderful revelation of himself. Almost she could have been the tiniest bit resentful of this . . .

And then she too slipped quietly into the unconsciousness of sleep. How long she slept she did not know. It may have been an hour . . . or a matter of moments. She was awakened by the banging of the broken shutter that Joel has set about mending that morning. It went through her with a nerve-racking insistency, until her body became numb and feelingless under the bludgeoning of that dreadful sound.

And the wind spoke to her . . . telling her wild and terrible things . . . telegraphing them to the sounding board of her unconscious self that translated those ominous whisperings and noises into words, heavy with portent . . .

And all that night she lay awake and listened to the wind.

Gravel in Your Shoe

YOU had to get your arms right down into the tub of suds, up to above the elbow. Without that it didn't feel somehow as if the whiteness of those drill suits would ever be able to emerge again in all their spotless, snowy, slick starchiness. You had to go deep down to get at the hidden dirt and grease spots. And if you thought that soap alone could do all the hard work for you, you'd pretty soon find yourself out of business.

She got their laundry work from folks not because they thought she was cheap, but because they knew she was good. The Chinese laundries couldn't do up a suit of white drill better. And she called for the laundry herself: Monday mornings. And delivered it herself; Thursday and Saturday afternoons. It was the personal contact – plus the quality of her work – that counted. Women liked to be able to talk about their men's white suits to the people who did them up. Just in case there was something for them to talk about. A button loose, a jacket-break not turned just right. A trouser seam or cuff that didn't please them. Women were fastidious about their men's white drill suits. And who could blame them. Not she. It was on account of this that she was able to continue in business.

During those periods when her man was out of work, she didn't worry. No need to worry. On what she earned they were able to carry on. She even managed to save a bit in the Post Office bank. She'd never known a day's sickness that she could remember. Except to bring her three children into the world. And you could hardly call *that* being sick.

She just kept singing away while she worked. Nearer My God To Thee. Jesus Lover Of My Soul. When Peace Like A River . . . not thinking so much about the words, as taking the soothing and comfort out of them. Singing because she found it made things lighter and brighter.

Not thinking over much about anything. She never forgot what someone had told her when she was a little girl, *it's not the mountain you're climbing that wears you down, but the gravel in your shoe.*

When the neighbours were bickering at each other, or gossiping, over their back fences, she just smiled to herself, singing some of the time.

Oh, she had troubles too. Who could imagine a woman who had lived thirty years in the world, and had kept her man faithful to her for ten years of that thirty – well, as good as she knew, and that's all that mattered – and had raised three children of her own, in all the perfection of smiling plumpness; could be without troubles. But like most people her troubles were little ones. Gravels in the shoe. Not mountains. Not really mountains.

When little Esme had had typhoid fever. That had looked like a mountain enough. With the child near to dying, and her man out of work again, and herself big with Ferdie at the time (that was the last one). Well it had looked mighty like a mountain. With all of them piled up like that, one on top of the other. And sometimes it felt like there was no use her trying to sing. Times when she couldn't bluff her face into making a smile. But they were gravels all the same, it turned out. Esme, near to death's door, pulled through, almost, it seemed, by a miracle. And although her man was out of work the best part of three months that time, a citrus packing house suddenly found they needed a foreman in the department where they made the crates. And although her man was a carpenter proper by trade, he was out of work so long he couldn't afford to feel himself too big to take the job. It turned out his foreman's job meant working sometimes ten, twelve hours a day, nailing crates together, with one boy to help him. But it was work. And poor people had no call to be proud. It was all damn-fool nonsense people thinking themselves too good for work.

True he had been handling his own gang of men on construction jobs, running up some of those swell new houses in St Andrew, and all. But he'd run into bad patches, bad breaks. Until he was glad of odd jobs here and there. Until at last this job at the citrus packing house, that wasn't much as to the money, but steady.

Her backyard adjoined that of Miss Matty, a garrulous old woman.
There was only a three-strand barbed wire fence between them.
An ackee tree that grew in her yard, and a custard apple in Miss
Matty's, formed the solid basis of their neighbourliness. Part of her
ackee tree hung over into Miss Matty's backyard, and part of Miss
Matty' custard apple into hers.

'Beg you few of your ackees,' said Miss Matty, ambling up to
the fence for a chat.

'Help you'self, Mam. They are on your side of the fence, in your
yard. You don't have to ask me, you know that.'

Just now she didn't feel like entering into conversation with Miss
Matty. In fact she hated the old woman's everlasting gossip. If she
only had the courage she would have got a man to chop down the
ackee tree, and so put an end once and for all to their
neighbourliness. But that she would never be allowed to hear the
last of it. All the people in the lane would talk about it for months.
They would build up around her such a legend of wickedness as
she would never be able to live down. Never be able to hold up
her head again among her neighbours. No one would speak to her.
Such an act of vandalism never would be forgiven or forgotten.
Their children would never be allowed to play with her children.
They would be considered outcasts as long as they lived there.

But how to erect an effective barrier between herself and the
garrulous old woman. There was no way. She must bear it to the
end. But cho! What was that to worry about. Just a gravel in the
shoe, that's all.

Recently they had become so neighbourly, in spite of all she could
devise to keep herself out of it, that Miss Matty had started talking
to her about him, telling her things she thought she ought to know
about where her man went evenings after he left home, and what
sort of company he was keeping, and how he was spending his
money, and upon what kind of women – and with her working
her fingers to the bone – and in short all the usual things. And
God's truth was she didn't want to listen.

She had built her life not upon barren gossip, and mistrust, and all things misbegotten; and chewing over the rag with herself, with him, nagging; or with the neighbours, airing her grievances. Not upon doubt, and upon imagined wrongs, or upon fears of what might come, or upon fretting him, or fretting herself in secret. She had built her life, her happiness, not upon these things. And maybe she was a fool, or not. What did it matter? But it mattered that to her the things she valued were above the cost of them. Whatever the cost to herself. That was what mattered. And this old woman maybe didn't know that, and there was no way it seemed to her of making her know. Because she didn't even know how to start telling her all this, all that her mind believed and accepted and rested upon. And she wouldn't understand even if she could bring herself to tell her.

If only she had the courage she would get a man to cut down that ackee tree.

She would cut off her right hand – well, her right leg, anyway – to preserve above the reach of adversity, above the clutch of doubt or fear, above the threat of what might come; that which to her was the burden as well as the song of being, of living. To preserve that whole, the whole thing in its entirety, that was what it meant to live. She had found out that herself. She had not learnt it laboriously, or stumbled upon it in the dark. She just knew it with the rest of knowledge about things, yourself, life, that is yours from the beginning, timelessly. It was hers from the beginning, timelessly. Nothing could shake, or destroy that out of her.

But this old woman now. What could she do about her? If she had courage sufficient unto herself to withstand their hate, their jibes, their speech deliberately and pointedly withheld, their sneers behind their hands, their talk among themselves, their innuendoes, their spite, their backbiting, all – she would get a man in tomorrow and cut down the ackee tree. But she knew herself in this wanting. She hadn't sufficient courage within herself. And she wanted only to be let alone. To live among them with love, a neighbour, but all the same to be let alone. To live her own life, to take that from it in which she conceived her abundant reward, letting well alone. To give to it that which she considered her privileged labour; with all gratitude for the abundance that was her portion. For the mountain under her feet, as well the gravel in her shoe. But leaving well alone.

About six o'clock he came in. The children were washed and tidied. Their loveliness, their plump smilingness, their shining, cherubic black faces that made them jewels to hang upon a gold chain; and no wit the less their tricks, their naughtiness, their small perverse humanness; was in itself proof of their obvious and conclusive rightness, and fitness, just as they were. Just as she plunged her arms deep in the tub to make the gleaming starched whiteness of those drill suits appear; because it was itself conclusive, proof of its rightness, its fitness in the scheme of things. Their proper whiteness and starchiness was. It just all seemed to fit. And that was conclusive enough for her.

And she didn't have to reason about it.

Just so it was right she should be setting out his supper on the table, and tending to his needs. With a smile upon her face that itself was proof, and the only outward proof, that she herself fitted into all this. And she too needed this proof. Without it something was lacking. So it was as she saw it, not learning it laboriously, or stumbling upon it in the dark. But knowing it a part of that knowledge about things that was living, and the capacity to live.

He sat down and ate his supper. Listening to her small conversation, without saying much himself. He never was one for saying much anyway. And she neither demanded nor expected it.

Did he notice things, she was happy. Because it made him happy, else why should he have noticed them? Did he seem to take no notice, to be taciturn, dull, restless, she didn't make that something to be sore about, to fret herself about, or fret him. Not so she conceived the pattern of living. She was a woman. Which woman didn't have her troubles? Her woman's troubles. But she wasn't going to tribulate over them. Men too, men had their troubles. Men's troubles and problems. If they both set up against each other, tribulating over their troubles, fretting each other to weariness that was worse than death, where was the sense of living? Was that living? Better they were dead than that.

She knew better than that. On the strength of that knowledge she had laid the foundation of her own life, and his, and theirs together. Of her own happiness, and his, and theirs together. On the strength of that knowledge that needed no proof of its rightness, its fitness, outside of itself. That was its own sufficient proof.

It was about seven o'clock when he went into the room and washed, and shaved, and changed his shirt. She came in after him, as soon as she had cleared the table of the supper things. She fetched him a clean towel, and told him where he would find his razor blades.

She told him about the Minorca hen that come out that morning with nine chickens. And about Mrs Aitken wanting to see him about making her a new dresser if he had the time. Sundays and after work.

As he took the towel from her hands, she knew him in some inner awareness, standing with her, her man. She didn't fret herself that he was going out. Possibly it might even be true he was gallivantin' with some other woman. What did it matter. Was that good and sufficient reason she should fret him and fret herself to that weariness that was worse than death?

She knew better than that. It was upon this knowledge, and all that went together with it, inseparably, that she had laid the very foundation of their life together. Complete, integrated, single, whole. Because they were held together by no such superficial bond as matrimony. They were just man and woman. Not married. She had no thought to ask him to marry her, as though she feared the dissolution of their life together, and sought to forge some artificial, conventional bond, that would be to join them together for all time. They were not man and wife in the naïve, conventional sense. But man and woman. Her man, his woman. A different thing.

She had not plagued him to marry her during all those ten years they had lived together, throughout all the vicissitudes they had equally shared. Because that in itself would destroy just this, this living bond, this bond of living between man and woman, that was to make them one, single, whole.

He plunged with a little fury of flailing arms and butting head into the starched white shirt, like a man going under water with his eyes shut and all, and coming up again, making a regular to-do about it.

She watched him, smiling. For conversation she told him about the new clothes-line that would reach from the ackee tree to the kitchen side. How they had charged her all of sixpence a foot more for the wire, and she was to consider herself lucky she got it at all. She told him what the man at the hardware store had said to her. 'Missis, soon there won't be wire enough to hang yourself with, if you had a mind to, much less clothes.' He was a regular joker, the man at the hardware store.

If only she had the courage she would cut down the ackee tree in the backyard. If ever *he* was to hear what was being said of him to her behind his back by that old woman next door, nothing would stop *him* cutting it down. More. He'd go all out and tell her why! But she couldn't do that. She dared not tell him. He must not hear.

She stood at the front door and watched him walk leisurely toward the gate, without ever once looking back. He was not the one to make a fuss over her. Kissing her when he didn't mean it. Playing up to her. Treating her like she was a child. Thank God for that too. She wouldn't want *that*, knowing him to be even then thinking about the other woman he was going to. Oh God! She wouldn't want him to be like that at all.

She closed the front door softly, and went back into the pantry where the children were, eating their supper, holding between their knees their blue and white porridge bowls. She would give them each a banana and send them out in front to play, till it was time for Ferdie to be put to bed, and Esme and Rebecca to prepare their home lessons for school.

If only she had the courage . . . Why couldn't they let her alone? She wanted to live among them like neighbours, with love. A woman had her troubles, her bread to eat in secret that no one might share. No one. Her life to live. The beginning and end of living, and all that lay between.

But oh Lord Jesus, sweet Jesus, if only they would let her alone.

Part IV

Look Out

SHE was at the gate, resting her arm on the top rail, her chin on her arms, looking out. Out being just any place that wasn't in. The moon rode high in the sky above great banks of clouds. Last night the moon was in eclipse. It was like someone had pulled a red curtain down over the face of the moon. But it was the moon all the same. Come clouds, come eclipse, it was all the same moon.

Somebody was calling to her from the house. That would be her sister-in-law. Her dear brother's wife. But she didn't pay no attention to her. She was a little cracked in the head. It was the moon. The moon made her come out from inside herself where she was locked away; inside her head, behind a smile that was like the double-blank in the box of dominoes. The moon made her come out from behind that dead smile and talk her head off. And shout her head off. But nobody paid no attention to her at all. Her brother's half-crazy wife.

She heard the sound of boots. Someone was coming slowly up the road. She didn't bother to turn her head to look. Just someone coming up the road. No matter.

She said out loud. Just thinking: 'Couldn't be gone ten yet.'

He stopped as though she had spoken to him. He was wearing khaki pants and a blue sport shirt. There was something about him that was lean and hard, and clean. Clean like he'd just come out of the tub. He stopped right under the street lamp that was before the gate and looked at his wrist-watch.

'Ten past,' he said.

She made a little sound with her tongue against her teeth.

But he was still there. Hesitating in his mind. Whether to stop and chat with her, or go on. She didn't give him any encouragement, or otherwise. She just kept on looking out, her chin resting upon her arms, her arms resting on the top of the gate.

'You waiting for someone,' he said. But he wasn't asking. He stood there still hestitating in his mind whether to stop and chat or to go on along his way.

Under the lamp post there was a diamond shaped sign that said 'Bus Stop'.

'The bus stops here,' he said. But he wasn't asking. He said it like he was reading the sign aloud, but to himself.

'It's going to rain,' he said. Lifting his face to the moon. 'Did you see the eclipse of the moon last night?' As you might say, 'read any good books lately?'

'Uh-huh,' she said.

Somebody was calling her from the house. Calling in a loud queer voice. He moved just one step. That took him one step nearer to the bus sign, so that he now stood on neutral ground. He might be waiting for the bus at the stop sign, or he might be talking to a girl at her gate, if the bus should come along and he didn't want to take it.

'That's just my sister-in-law,' she said. 'I don't pay no mind to her.' Lifting a foot to the lowest rail of the gate, but without otherwise changing her position.

He lit a cigarette carelessly and looked up at the moon. He stood for a while like that, not saying anything, just looking up.

The clouds were banked up high against the moon, so that she looked wild and stormy tonight, and as though filled with a great unrest.

But cho! it was only the moon. Always the moon. The rest was trimmings. They didn't mean anything.

The man said: 'It's going to rain.' Blowing out a cloud of smoke. To him the trimmings meant something.

She wanted to laugh.

'What you are? A weather-prophet?'

'Them clouds,' he said. 'See them dark ones underneath like? They say rain!'

'Ain't you smart,' she mocked.

'That's right,' he said, without his face changing.

The man was a fool. She would snub him. She would wait for him to say something to her, and she would take pains to snub him.

Besides it wasn't right she should be here chatting with him. At any moment her brother might ride up on his bicycle. He would scold her, inside. Though who could say she was in fact chatting with anyone? Wasn't her fault there was a bus stop just outside their gate. Wasn't she put it there.

She said: 'Weren't you going for a walk?'

He said without looking at her: 'I was.'

'I changed my mind now,' he said. 'I'm waiting for the bus.'

Her foot on the rail started of itself bouncing her knee up and down. Like she might have been hushing a baby to bye-bye. She was doing that without thinking about it.

But he saw it out of the corner of his eye. Without looking around. Saw her bare knee bouncing. It was a pretty knee – to pass up just like that. She might be waiting for someone, sure. But all the same where he was standing was public thoroughfare. He might be going some place, or not. Wasn't anybody's business. She didn't have to answer back if she didn't want. He could say, it's going to rain, without talking to anyone. Just saying it looked like it was going to rain.

The three children had been put to bed long ago. Her brother's children. Couldn't be anything she could do that her sister-in-law kept calling, calling at her. She just wouldn't pay any mind to her. Let her call. It was the moon. The moon was full tonight. Last night there had been an eclipse, and it looked just like someone had drawn a red blind down over the face of the moon. And bit by bit the blind had lifted. Until the last time she had looked at it, it was just like someone had broken a piece out of the moon somewhere near the top.

A few people passed in the street. She heard them come and go without looking at them. Except when they passed her line of vision looking straight out before her, she didn't see them. Two three bicycles went by, but nothing to make her take her mind off what she was thinking about – nothing.

She wasn't thinking about anything tonight. She wasn't waiting for anyone either. Leastways she didn't know anyone she *could* be waiting for. Except it was that she was waiting for her brother to come home? And why *should* she be waiting for her brother to come home? She was just tired of staying indoors doing nothing. With a crazy woman for company. She was just leaning against the gate, looking out, doing nothing. Thinking about nothing.

Sometimes it got so bad sitting indoors with only her sister-in-law for company, that she wanted to put her hands up to her head and scream!

But she wasn't going to do that. She wasn't going to let it get her that way. The loneliness. The emptiness of everything. Ever since she had left home and come to live with her brother in the city. Because his wife was that way again, bringing them into the world faster than she could look after them.

If she let it get her, someday she would be getting like her sister-in-law. All shut inside her head. Her face blank. Her eyes. That fixed dead smile. All like the double-blank in the box of dominoes.

She hadn't known it was going to be like this in the city. Else she wouldn't have left home in the first place. Short of them hog-tying her and dragging her here. She hadn't known her brother meant to lock her inside a house and not want her to see anyone from outside, and not want her to have any friends or go anywhere. *If* she had known!

Maybe he was just one of those fresh guys. The city, she was warned, was full of them. Or maybe he was a married man himself with a family of three squalling children, and his wife that way again. But cho! That didn't bother her. She wasn't even giving him a thought. That way.

'Ever seen a man climb right up one of them electric line poles?' he said, looking at her.

'No,' she said. Was he trying to be funny?

Ever seen a man climbing a pole! What was he coming with now. What did he take her for? A fool? What was his line? What was he getting at? Ever seen a man climbing a pole, indeed! What sort of fast one did he think he was pulling out from up his sleeve now. What was he getting around to? What was he coming with now?

Cho! It must be one of those jokes he was trying to tell her. Just one of those fresh guys. Trying to get fresh with her.

'What you talking about, a man climbing a pole?' she said.

'That's me,' he said. 'Linesman.'

'Linesman?' she said.

'Linesman. That's what they call us. Wire-monkeys. We look after the lines.'

So. That was it. He was telling her about himself.

'So what?' she said. Doing her stuff. Pretending she was indifferent.

'You ought to see me going up one of them poles,' he said.

'Why?' she said. Like what.

'With my steel spurs on,' he said.

Steel spurs! What next. What did he take her for, anyway?

'Steel spurs,' he said again. Looking at her.

At the sides of his boots, he said, for gripping the pole. How else could you climb a pole, he said, if you come to think about it.

But she didn't say anything. Just kept on as she was, leaning against the gate looking out. Her bare knee kept on bouncing like all the time she didn't know she was doing it.

So he was a wire-monkey. He climbed poles! He did that for a living. She could see him in her mind's eye climbing up that pole across the way hand over hand – like a monkey – without thinking about it. Wondering how soon her brother might be happening along.

He too was silent. Thinking his own thoughts.

Why didn't he say something? She was suddenly and unaccountably annoyed with him. What did he think he was doing just standing there pulling at his cigarette in a self-satisfied way, like the world and everything in it belonged to him tonight, not saying anything. Just taking it in. Just letting things come to him, and taking it all in. He had a nerve!

She wanted to hear more about him. About this queer occupation of his, anyway. Fancy doing *that* for a living! Or was he just taking her along? Trying to get fresh with her?

'What you do when you climb the pole?' she said.

'Oh, things. Fix the lines. Put in new ones. Tend them in general.'

That made sense at least. The lines *would* need fixing. Somehow she had never thought of it before. What a lot of queer occupations there must be in the world. So many queer jobs to be done. Somebody had to do them. It was the same all over the world. Her job for instance. Taking care of her sister-in-law, her brother's children. That was one of them. Somebody had to do it. That was why her brother didn't want her to have any friends. Because he wanted her to do that job. He had a long head to his body; her brother.

It was dangerous work too. He might easily get killed fooling with them wires. They were charged with electricity. She knew that. She could see him, without thinking about it, atop one of them poles, caught somehow in amongst the wires, burning up.

'Isn't it dangerous?' she said.

'Not worth speaking of,' he said. 'That is, if you know what you're doing. Them wires carry a powerful lot of volts. If I was to tell you how much you wouldn't believe me. Some of them. Could kill you quicker than thinking. If you don't mind your step.'

She said: 'I should *think* so!' And he looked at her quickly, and smiled.

So then: 'That don't seem to me much of a way for a man to make his living,' she said.

He laughed at that. Just laughed. As though he was saying to himself, well *she* didn't know anything. A girl like that!

The bus came up to the stop then. Somebody got off. Two people. A girl first, and a man after her. They went on down the road. She saw them without looking at them. The bus went on again.

'Weren't you waiting for the bus?' she said.

'Did I say I was?' he said.

She made no answer.

'Maybe I changed my mind,' he said. Without looking at her.

'You live here,' he said. But he wasn't asking. He had a way of saying things like that. Like he was just thinking out aloud.

She said nothing.

'Maybe you would care to go for a walk,' he said. Looking at her. 'Not tonight,' he said, before she could say anything. 'Some other night.' And left it like that.

'No! No!' she said quickly, shaking her head.

'Why?' he said.

'Don't ask me why. It can't be, that's why.'

He just laughed.

'Maybe you'll change your mind,' he said.

'No! No!' she said.

'All right,' he said. 'I was just saying. Anyone can change their mind.'

A bicycle came round the bend up the road. She knew, without knowing, that it was her brother coming home.

'You must go now,' she said, quickly. 'Please go now.'

He looked at her. His face started to laugh, but dropped it. It was as though he understood everything, without her saying it.

'Your husband, eh?'

'No, my brother. You must go now. Please!'

In those few words he understood everything. More than enough to go on. Things she hadn't meant to let out to him. Had let out without knowing!

You must go now! Please! That made it right with him. That told him something besides. That already there was something between them. Something tacit, and implicit. He wasn't slow in these things.

'Goodnight, then. Be seeing you,' he said, without looking at her.

With his hands in his pockets he sauntered off carelessly. A young man taking the air.

'What you doing here? Who you waiting for?' her brother questioned suspiciously as he came up.

'Nothing. Nobody.' she answered.

'You should be inside,' he said. 'No sense to stand at the gate looking out for nothing.'

The wind died down. Suddenly there was no wind at all. Not so much as would stir a leaf. A great drop of rain fell *plop* against her cheek. She put her hand up to her cheek and took it away wet.

'It's going to rain!' she said, looking at her hand, as though she had made a wonderful discovery.

'Get inside,' he said, harshly. 'Get inside now. You have no business standing out here like that, for nothing.'

She moved slowly to do his bidding. As though it was his will not hers that moved the muscles in her body. That moved her legs along. But her mind. That was not his. She looked up at the face of the moon. Last night it was in eclipse. Tonight it was restless and driven, with great black clouds driving across the face of it.

And suddenly she wanted to cry. But not here, where he could see her. Inside in her own little room. Where no one could see her. She would just put her head down and cry. And not because she was sad. And not because she was happy. She only knew she wanted to put her head down and cry and cry her eyes out. And all for nothing.

Red Dirt Don't Wash

HE stood awkwardly, shifting his weight from one foot to the other, looking through the open pantry window with the dancing eyes of a boy about to receive a treat of good things. But it wasn't the jam tarts that the maid, Miranda, was taking hot from the oven and putting in a dish that held his gaze, rapt. It was Miranda herself, flicking her fingers smartly and putting them to her mouth as the hot baking tin burnt them.

Her trim figure in her blue uniform, chic, neat-fitting, made his eyes swim in his head. It was as though whenever she was in sight he couldn't take his eyes off her. She ravished his senses. And simple country yokel that he was he didn't know how to set about making a girl like Miranda. For Miranda was city-bred, and house-broke, and all the things that he wasn't. She had training. She had refinement, culture. She knew how to lay a table all by herself. Things like that. She knew all the tableware, all the silver, by name. She could tell them over to you, without even stumbling once. He had often helped her polish them, so he knew.

She knew which was a cake fork from a fish fork. She knew a cake server from a cheese server. She knew a tea plate from a breakfast plate, and which one of the shiny mugs was a coffee percolator, and which was for hot water, and which for cream. There wasn't anything she didn't know.

And she had let him help her after his work in the garden was over. She had let him stand near as near to her over the kitchen sink and wash dishes . . . and feel the presence of her, the delicious, maddening nearness of her go through him like sharp knives, like red hot needles. He could get the smell of her in his nostrils, standing that near to her; like you get the smell of a ripe fruit in your nostrils when you bite it! She smelt like a lady. Just like any lady. He wondered what it was that gave her that delicious, wonderful, ravishing perfume to her body; and so he had been tempted to stand on tiptoe outside the crack in the window of her room, where the gummed paper just didn't cover it quite, and take a good long look at her . . . one day after she had come out from the servants' shower bath. What he had seen had devastated him. He had come away feeling dizzy, faint; as though something was happening inside him, in his stomach.

He had seen all her loveliness in the nude. For one devastating instant he had held within his dull, unimaginative eye, all her loveliness that was without blemish; and his heart was like a leaping fish held in the hand.

But he knew now what it was that gave her body that delicious smell, that mounted to his nostrils like incense, and held his senses within a hazy sort of swoon, and gave him that dry feeling in his throat, and that queer feeling in his stomach. It was powder!

She took powder from a large red tin and dusted it all over her body. Not just dabbing it on her face alone, like other girls did, but all over her body!

Such luxury! Such expensiveness! It made his head reel.

Made him aware of his own grossness, his own inferiority, his own lack of polish and refinement. Made him aware of his own soiled and patched clothes, and his own large bare feet, his own rough red skin, which seemed as though the red dirt of his native Clarendon hills had come there to stay, and couldn't ever wash off.

When his work was done in the garden, when he had washed down the car, and rubbed it down with a chamois cloth until it shone, she would let him carry the pan in which she washed napkins and doilies and table-runners and handkerchiefs, and small things like that (for you must understand that Miranda was no ordinary servant, but a lady's maid. She was not a cook, though she made delicious pastries. Not a washer-woman, although she was entrusted with the washing of doilies and the table-runners and the cushion covers and the table napkins and the handkerchiefs and the silk stockings, and dainty things like that). She would let him carry

91

the pan with its heaping foam of white suds from the sink under the standpipe in the backyard to the deal table on the back verandah; and he would just stand and watch her, her arms up to the elbows in suds. Now and then she would look up from her work and smile at him, and he grinned back at her all the time.

He learnt a lot from just standing around talking and joking with her; and helping her through her pantry chores sometimes.

He told her about the place he came from. All about his people up in the mountains. And the ways in which their ways were different from the ways of the people who lived in towns. And she laughed alot. She was a great one for laughing.

'They are simple, jealous folk, but really the kindest people in the world. We understand each other. We know what makes a man or a woman happy, and what makes them mad. All the people in my district get along together like one big family.'

'My! And I suppose all the girls and the men work together in the fields? Don't tell me that! Really?'

'It just come natural for everybody to pitch in and do whatever work there is to be done – whether in the fields, or about the yard, or in the house – it's all the same. But mostly the men do the heavier work. And women in the family way don't do any but the slightest things.'

'You don't say!' She squealed with laughter.

'They say,' she remarked, twinkling up at him, provocatively, 'that all the people are red – like you. Is that true?'

He just grinned back at her for answer.

'Even the dirt is red. All red dirt. They say the people's skins take its colour from the dirt, if they live there long enough – all their lives, I suppose.' She frowned a little, flicking soapsuds from her forearms and hands. 'They say the red dirt gets on them, and even *inside* them, under their skins, and just stays there.

She looked at him quizzically.

'Don't know 'bout that. I 'spects it's so! Never give it no thought before.'

'It's true. For no matter where you meet a mountain man you can always know him. I guess it must be true – that red dirt don't wash.'

Once or twice she let him walk home with her, where she stayed with her cousin who was another kind of maid – an office maid – because she got along better with gentlemen, they said.

But always she led him through back lanes, and down through a dry gully course, and always she parted with him at a certain spot some little way from the house. And he never questioned her. He never thought to question anything she did.

He knew this girl was right – just right in everything she did or said. Almost a lady. Much too good for him, just a country boy. Big and clumsy and awkward and halting in speech and gestures. Almost a living caricature of a country boy, he was so bad. But he knew also that he wanted her, even though she was miles too good for him. And at first it didn't trouble him at all, the thought of wanting her so badly. But after a bit it got to haunting him at nights. Days and nights, so that he got no rest from the thought of her that was sweet torture to him.

He would lie in his bed and remember every sprightly word and vivid gesture of hers. How she looked at him, looking up sideways, like a little bird, and laughing in his face. Well, a girl didn't look at a fellow like that unless she – she kind of liked him. A bit.

He remembered how she put out her hand once and touched his arm – and grabbed hard hold of his arm around the bicep muscles and said 'My!', admiringly. Meaning how hard and strong he was. He remembered how she let a clothes-pin fall down his back once, and laughing that squealing laugh of hers, ran her hand down after it, and fetched it up slowly from way down at his waist – skylarking – while he just sat still and let her do what she would with him. He remembered all that; and it was as though things were going on inside him all the time, in his blood, secretly.

Once or twice he saw her walking out with nice looking young men – chauffeurs, and such. He envied them. Not alone because she was walking out with them, but because of something they had that he lacked. A poise, a certain assurance that was almost swagger. Shoes on their feet. The way they wore their clothes.

He had never worn shoes in his life, but once. Once, when he was about seventeen, his Gran'pa had bought him a pair of yellow boots to wear Sundays. They were grand boots. They must have cost a pile of money. He wore them once to church. And that was enough. His feet inside boots didn't feel like his at all. He lost possession of them, and they behaved as though they knew it.

He let them go cheap to a boy he knew from the neighbouring district, about his size. The other fellow got a real bargain. They were grand boots. But he didn't care. He bought him a goat with the money. Now there were six goats the last time he heard from home, and more coming along. He didn't care about the boots. Boots wore out and got old so you had to throw them away. But a goat gave you more and more goats. He liked goats. Now there was something he knew about.

One evening as he walked home with her – they were halfway through the dry gully course when he made bold enough to carry out the desperate scheme he had been turning over slowly, methodically in his mind all along – he suddenly blurted out:

'I seen you walking out with fellows.'

She looked up at him quickly.

Her eyes, he noticed, were bright like stars, her lips slightly parted, as though she were panting from walking too fast; but they had been coming along slowly, saying nothing, mostly; their bodies just touching, or almost touching, in the dark.

He said, stopping suddenly and looking down at her face.

'I would like for you to come out with me, once in a while. Eh?'

'How? Where?'

'Movies?' It was a bold gesture. He had never been to a movie in his life . . . now he was asking this girl to go with him. Just like that.

Unconsciously he was taking on to himself some of the easy swagger of the young men he'd seen Miranda with.

He said, coming closer to her. 'What say we go to a movie Sat'day night? You'n me. Eh?'

She looked up at his face . . . and away . . . and down at his feet.

Suddenly, unexpectedly, she burst out laughing. She just fell on the bank and squealed with laughter. She *was* a one for laughing!

But it did something to him. For one thing it made him lose all his recently acquired swagger; for another it made him all of a sud-

den fiercely resolved within his mind to make her take it all back.
To make her look at him as she looked at her natty young men.
Plus the special look she gave *him* – that said as plain as anything
that she could like him – and more than a bit.

'All right,' he said, in a terrible, calm voice. 'I know I'm not
good enough for you. But all the same I love you, see.'

She stopped laughing immediately. She put the back of her hand
to her mouth.

'Adrian,' she said. 'I – I'm not laughing – at what you think.
I'm just laughing like – oh you don't understand about women,
or you would know.'

He was silent for a while, chewing on this. Of course she was
right. He didn't understand about women, either. Not her kind.
She was miles above him. She would take *some* understanding. Of
a sudden he felt great humility, standing before her . . . great
humility, and with it a great resolve.

The very next day he put the first part of his resolve into effect.
He asked for time off in the afternoon and went to town to one
of the big stores where they sold shoes and things.

'How much for the yellow ones in the window?' he asked, after
the man at the store had showed him half-a-dozen pairs from the
shelves.

'Now there's a pair of shoes for you! Genuine vici kid. You can't
do better than that at any price, anywhere. It's marked twenty-
five shillings. We sold the lot before this at twenty-seven and six.
But I tell you what. Now I'm doing the best I can for you. It isn't
like I'd do this for everyone. But I'll put them in for you – special
– for twenty-two and elevenpence.

'I'll take them,' said Adrian, without hesitation.

All that money for a pair of shoes. But he didn't mind that a
bit. They were genuine vici kid. Goat skin leather, he knew that
too. You could buy two goats, let alone the skins, for twenty-two
and eleven. But he didn't mind that a bit. She put powder on all
over her. He seen it himself. He knew!

Came Saturday night; and to Adrian it seemed none too soon,
either.

He put on his best Sunday clothes of blue serge, and his yellow shoes. He looked down at his feet and admired the gleaming shine of them.

He went round by the back of the tennis court from the garage, through the little enclosed vegetable garden, to the back porch, where he knew he would find her, his shoes creaking faintly across the grass. His feet felt as though they were taking him places. This was different to just walking. Just walking you set your feet down, one before the other, without thinking about it. He'd heard about a man walking on a clothes-line wire high above the ground. He'd often thought about it, wondering how it felt. He didn't anymore after that night. He knew.

The family had dined, and had gone out in the car. He knew just where she would be, what doing, and that she would be alone.

When she saw him, she just stood looking at him for a time. Then she suddenly burst out laughing, as though she wouldn't stop.

She said: 'Where you all dressed up going to, Adrian?' Like that.

He said, coming up close to her: 'We're steppin' out.'

'My! Who an' you?'

'You an' me. Remember? You said if I got myself some shoes . . . remember? Well, I got them. They cost a heap of money too. But I don't give it a thought.'

He swelled out his chest. He was almost as big as a barrel around. For a moment she looked at him with slightly troubled eyes. His body looked so strong and fine, beneath all the marks of the country lad on him. The awkwardness. You could see at a glance his flesh was good and strong. Her eyes sort of misted over a bit. For a moment though. And then they dropped to his feet again.

'What's the matter, don't they look all right?'

'Sure. They're swell. They must have cost a pile of money, I bet.'

And she burst out laughing.

At first he didn't understand, and he started laughing too, with his hearty country lad's guffaw. And then he saw her face; saw how she looked at his feet, and looked up and laughed again. And suddenly the laughter died out of him. Leaving him, as it were, standing there foolishly, with his mouth open, staring at her.

She said, curiously enough: 'Don't make me laugh!' gasping.

'But what – why – what's the matter with them?'

'Nothing, big boy. The shoes are fine. But they're not yours, that's all. They don't fit you, see?'

'They's a bit tight. But my feet'll get used to them after a spell.'

'That's where you are wrong. They never will. They'll always look just what they are — a pair of shoes carrying your feet around. All your life you've never worn shoes. You know that's true.'

He nodded.

'You can't educate them feet to shoes, big boy. Not as long as you live. You'll always *feel* as though you were wearing shoes, and you'll *look* just the way you feel. Always. No, it's no good. Better take them off now. Perhaps if you clean the soles a bit they might even take them back from you at the store where you bought them.'

'But I don't want them to take them back. They're mine. You know why I got them,' he said, looking down at them self-consciously. 'It was all for you.'

At that she burst out laughing again.

'Do you think I'm going out with you, in *them*?' she demanded scornfully. It was no use. No use at all thinking about sparing his feelings. He just didn't have sense enough for a child. Nothing short of this could make him understand. It was a pity, but none of her cooking, she was sure.

'I get you,' he said, slowly. 'I'm not good enough for you. Oh I know it. Still, you said if I got myself some shoes, like . . .'

'Don't take it hard, big boy.' She laid a hand on his arm. But for a moment only, then she took it away. 'I tell you what,' she said in a low, husky voice. Perversely the firm, strong, clean touch of his flesh stung her like nettles; went driving with sharp pangs through her, stirring something in her blood. 'Tomorrow night we'll go for a walk. I know a place we can go where nobody'll be around.' A pause. 'That's a promise, now.'

But he remained for a space, looking away, saying nothing. Then he turned slowly, painfully away, with the unaccustomed pain of walking in tight shoes. But he was resolved upon this thing. He was going to walk them in . . . going to walk those darned feet of his in. He'd do it if it broke his heart, if it killed him.

After walking about a mile, he came to a lonely spot on the road. He didn't even know where he was, but he didn't care.

He sat down on the side of the road and pulled off his shoes. He took each foot between his hands and chafed it gently, wriggling his toes until they felt like his own again.

She was leading him on, she was. Playing him for a sucker . . . all the time laughing at him, and carrying on with other fellows . . . and laughing at him behind his back.

He felt in his pocket for his clasp knife and opened and tested the blade passing it along the ball of his thumb. There was a cold, still, sullen look in his eyes. Deadly like anger burned down the glowing coals of a still white heat.

What she wanted to make of him a blooming Cinderella for? Just so she could laugh at him.

He lifted his head and stared blankly up at the cold stars. There was nothing there. Beyond them the sombre mountains. They reminded him of his own mountains that seemed so far away, almost unreal – veiled as with a mist – and the mist was in his own eyes – trying to see beyond the St Andrew hills, beyond the stars, horizon; space limitless like that.

He tested the edge of the blade against the ball of his thumb. And it was right. What she want to make of him a blooming Cinderella for?

He took the shoes, one at a time, and cut them into thin strips – all but the soles, which, because of their toughness he just cut anyway.

Back there he belonged, where there was red dirt everywhere, and people didn't go around wearing shoes. Red dirt everywhere, on the tilled land as far as the eyes could see, and on the faces and bare arms and legs of men and women. Good, clean red dirt that he loved, that was the symbol of home to him, and more. Clean, happy faces that he loved, that were all frankness and homeliness. All that went for cleanness and wholeness. It was clean, the red dirt of his land, the place of his birth.

He looked down at the jagged strips of leather in his hand, and his face became wonderfully luminous. He even smiled.

They were good shoes. Genuine vici kid. He paid twenty-two and elevenpence for them at the store.

Part IV

The Ranger

EPHRAIM came to the district as an itinerant labourer, but he rented a piece of land and stayed on, on account of Mabel. He fell in love with Mabel, the ranger's daughter, one day when he came upon her walking through the field. At that time he lived in one room of the wooden barracks to which the men from his district were allotted. But that arrangement only lasted for a time because the property had need of more labourers to keep the banana plantation cleaned and pruned.

It might be said that Ephraim fell in love with Mabel at first sight, but there were other meetings, of course. There was something in her bold black eyes when she looked at him that gave Ephraim cause to pursue his dream of having Mabel.

He owned a plot of land with a shack on it, and a cow, way back in his own district. But a man cannot live on an acre planted in cassavas and sweet potatoes, with only a couple of hens and a cow, and there was no work to be had in his district except after heavy rain when the Public Works wanted men to mend the roads. So he sold his lot and cow, gave his hens to an old aunt who had always been fond of him, and came and rented this plot of land which was near to the plantation where he could get work for perhaps six months in the year. And Mabel came and lived with him.

Three months hadn't gone by, however, when they went and got married properly at the little Baptist church in the village.

In the course of the first three years of their married life Mabel bore him two children, girls. One was called Mabeline for her mother, and the other Suzan for Ephraim's old aunt.

Ephraim was a quiet easy-going sort of chap, and Mabel was a robust smiling industrious girl. As time went by they prospered.

First they got a goat, and soon they had six or seven goats. Someone gave Mabel a little pig of a litter of thirteen that the mother-sow had died and left. Mabel fed the little pig with goat's milk from a bottle with a leather nipple that Ephraim made to fit it. The little pig grew into a big pig, and by the time it was ready to go to the butcher their herd of goats had increased to thirteen.

'We could take the money for the pig and buy us a calf,' said Ephraim to Mabel. He wanted to have a cow, somehow it gave a man a feeling of security to have a cow of his own, it made him feel settled and not just a wanderer on the face of the earth. They also rented a piece of land in the backlands of the property on which Ephraim worked and there they planted yams, plantains, cocoas, and other provisions, so they could have plenty to eat all during the year. Altogether the future looked quite rosy for them.

One day as Mabel was going to the spring for water she came upon the prostrate body of a man lying across the pass. At first she thought the man was dead, but upon closer examination she discovered that he was only drunk. Even as she looked he seemed to be coming out of his drunken coma. She went on down to the spring and filled her pail with water. But as she stooped down to lift it to her head she felt a queer feeling come over her, a curious combination of nausea and fear. It affected her so powerfully that she gave a loud scream and turned her head to look fearfully behind her. She saw the drunken man staggering down the pass. She was suddenly and unaccountably afraid of him. It seemed to her that he was the personification of her fear. Unreasoningly she put her apron up to her face and ran blindly past him up the pass leaving her pail filled with water at the side of the spring.

She did not stop running until she reached home.

'What is the matter with you, Mabel?' said Ephraim, coming out into the yard and catching sight of her troubled face.

'I have seen a duppy,' she said, collapsing on the doorsetp and breathing with short gasps. Her body shook all over as she spoke, so that Ephraim looking down at her with bewilderment and commiseration could see that something dreadful had happened. But he considered that it would not do to encourage her in such superstitious beliefs.

'A duppy!' said Ephraim incredulously. 'You mean you seen a duppy for sure?'

Mabel only nodded her head.

'But that is nonsense,' said Ephraim, sharply. 'Who ever heard of anyone seeing a duppy in broad daylight, supposing there is such things as duppies at all.'

'Where did you see this duppy then,' he asked her; and she told him. 'Down by the spring.' And then after a bit she told him everything that had happened, how she had gone down to the spring for water, and how she had seen the dead man lying across the pass, and how she had seen the body twitch and move after a bit, and thought it was only a drunken man fallen asleep in the pass. How she had gone on down to the spring, and had suddenly been overcome with that dreadful sensation, 'as though me belly turned over inside me, an' me head growed,' she said.

And Ephraim said, come, they would go on down back to the spring together and he would see this thing for himself. At first Mabel did not want to do that, nor for Ephraim to go down to the spring alone, either; but after some persuasion she agreed to accompany him.

When they got to the spring there was no man to be seen, but there was her pail filled to the brim with water, standing at the side of the pass exactly as she had left it.

'I don't understand it,' said Ephraim, scratching his head. He wanted to believe Mabel's story, and had come fully expecting to see the drunken man perhaps sitting by the side of the spring wetting his head with water.

'He must have gone up the pass and way over the hill,' said Ephraim, musingly, although he knew perfectly well that he couldn't very well have done that in the time he had, unless he had run like a mongoose all the way.

'Or he may have followed the spring and gone down into the pasture yonder,' he said.

But Mabel said nothing. And suddenly a Mountain-Witch bird flew over their heads and gave voice to its harsh cry.

'I think I'll just go and take a look-see,' said Ephraim.

But Mabel clutched him by the arm and cried, 'No, no. I am

not going to let you go a foot out of my sight.' And then she said, coaxingly, 'Come, let's go on back to the house.'

So he took the pail on his shoulder and they went back up the pass together, and Mabel was so weak and shaken she could hardly walk.

It did not take Mabel many days to get over her shock, however, and soon her fears, and indeed the very incident itself, were quite forgotten. They never spoke of it again, and she was not reminded of it until one day she came face to face with the man she had seen that day at the spring. He was quietly playing dominoes with some men of the district at one end of the counter in the Chinaman's shop where the two roads meet.

For some reason unknown even to herself she conceived a curious reticence about the matter. In fact she didn't tell Ephraim, or anyone else for that matter, that she had seen her 'duppy' in the flesh playing dominoes in the Chinaman's shop at the Cross Roads.

The man was a stranger to the district and he had come here looking for work. He got work on the plantation pruning bananas. He was a strange man, however, and he never did mix much with the other labourers on the plantation. Very soon his industriousness, his aloofness, the stern way he had with people, attracted the attention of the overseer who was on the lookout for a new ranger, because the first one, Mabel's father, was getting old and could not move about as he should, on account of asthma and a touch of rheumatism in the joints.

So one pay-day the people on the plantation were told that this man, whose name was Thomas, was the new ranger. It was soon apparent that none of the people who worked on the plantation liked him, and many feared and hated him. There was something about him that just repulsed everyone. But the overseer thought that was all to the good.

But after a time even the overseer came to feel the man's repulsiveness, some quality about him that literally gave him the shivers, made him uncomfortable in the presence of the other. And yet he couldn't explain it even to himself.

One morning Thomas came into the overseer's office without knocking. He just looked up from his account books to see the man standing over him. He had his knapsack over his shoulder and his machete under his arm.

'What is it, Thomas?' said the overseer, somewhat sharply.

The ranger gave him a queer look out of his fish-like eyes, and held out his hand, palm upward, toward him. There was some money in his palm.

'What's this?'

'Some bananas got blown down in the high winds last night. I sold them this morning to a man who came around in a truck to buy rejected fruit.'

The overseer looked at him frowningly.

'You shouldn't have done that. You know all bananas that leave this plantation should be taken to the fruit shed and checked.'

'I thought I would save the expense of heading them in from the field. I am sorry if I have done wrong,' said the man gruffly. 'They were bruised fruit. I only thought of saving on the pay-bill, that's all.'

'Well, don't let it happen again,' said the overseer, taking the money and checking it against a slip of paper the ranger gave him containing a count of the stems.

'Don't let this sort of thing happen in the future, Thomas,' he said again, as the ranger was going out.

And it never did.

But people started stealing bananas from the plantation, cutting them the night before buying-day, and this worried the overseer and the ranger, both. And although many a watch was set, yet no thief was ever caught.

'I know for sure who is stealing the bananas,' said Mabel to Ephraim. And he said, quickly, 'Who?'

'It's none other than that ranger himself,' she said.

And he said, gruffly: 'You don't go talking careless all over the place, all you do. Mind your tongue.'

So she didn't say anything more about it, because she didn't like it when he spoke crossly to her.

It seemed for days like something was worrying Ephraim, and it made Mabel very unhappy to see him in this condition of mind.

Ephraim felt that it was on account of his seriousness why she was unhappy, so one evening after supper, after the children had been put to bed, he laid an arm about her waist and led her out into the yard and they walked about a bit, lover-like in the moonlight, and presently he made her sit down beside him on the doorstep, and he started telling her stories that he had heard as a boy. And he told her stories of his own family and of funny things that had happened in his district, and she laughed very much, for Ephraim, when he had a mind to, could tell a good story.

She laughed about the old woman who was so mean that she fed her children on bananas and sweet cassava only, never so much as a piece of pickled fish did they have to eat. She would buy a piece of salt mackerel at the shop and she would cook it nicely and set it on a plate in the middle of the table, and she would let the children smear their food on the mackerel, and that was all. Then she ate the mackerel all herself, and when she went to the field to work, for she was a hard-working body, she took what was left of the mackerel with her wrapped in a plantain leaf and some old newspaper, because she knew that if she left it at home the children would fall to and eat it off, every bit. The old woman had a cow which she loved very much because it gave her milk every day, and she drank a lot of milk, not alone because she was a very greedy old woman, but also because she had to do to keep herself strong as a she-mule to do all the work she had to do to keep her family going, and without a man in the place.

One day the old woman went to sleep under a tree in her field because she was tired, and also because she had eaten much and the sun was hot. She always took the cow with her to the field and tethered it with a long rope, also it had a little bell about its neck that she bought for elevenpence at a church fair, for the old woman was very much attached to the cow, even though she was a dirty old woman who went around in rags because she didn't believe in spending money buying clothes when there was food to be bought. All her children went around in rags, too.

As she lay under the tree and slept she had a dream of heaven, and warm caresses, and angels and bells, soft tinkling bells of silver and gold, and she smiled blissfully in her dream because she was so happy.

She came awake at last with the sweet breath of the cow blowing gently against her face. She sat up and looked around her, a bit dazed still with sleep; the wind blew now and she shivered with cold. She had a strange feeling as though everything wasn't quite real, and as it used to be. She looked around her, and it was the same old field in which she had laboured for so many years. But still the feeling that something was different, persisted. And now she looked down at herself and found that she was born-naked. The cow had eaten up her rags clean off her, down to the last piece; and the cow had done that on account of the salt from the mackerel it had tasted when it had come up and licked her. There was that delicious salty taste of mackerel all over her rags, and they were all so rotten with wear that they came off her without even disturbing her slumber.

Mabel laughed very much when Ephraim told her the story of the old woman and the cow, and she begged for more.

But Ephraim was tired now and he wanted to go to bed, and for her to come to bed with him.

'I don't remember any more funny ones tonight,' said Ephraim. And then he laughed and said, 'There is a story about a dead man who came alive again.'

'A funny story?' said Mabel.

'Maybe,' he said. Then he said, 'That's not the sort of story to tell you at night. It might give you bad dreams.'

'But you will tell me sometime?' she said, and she made him promise that he would tell her that story another day. And he pulled her gently to him and caressed her. And she said, laughing against his shirt, 'I feel just like the old woman dreaming under the tree, with your hands on me, only thank God it is not just a dream, and you are not a cow.' For she was feeling very happy tonight, happier than she had been for many many a day; and Ephraim was feeling happy too. And so they went to bed.

But the next morning she said to him again: 'I know who is stealing the bananas off this place.' And again he spoke sharply to her: 'Shut you mouth!' he said. And the old unhappy look came into his eyes again.

When he left her and went to the field she sat and cried in her apron; but not for long for she was a sensible young woman, and she had bright spirit.

But all the same she felt she knew more about this man Thomas, than did anyone else in the district. And somehow, in some occult way, her knowledge made her afraid.

One afternoon as she was coming from their provision field with a basket full of yams and sweet potatoes on her head, she came face to face with him, coming round a bend in the pass. For a moment they just stood there looking at each other. There was deadly antagonism in that exchange of glances. He stood in the middle of the pass, so that she could not pass him unless she were to set her bare feet down on the sharp rock-stones on the one side, or climb a steep bank on the other, and she determined in her heart that she wouldn't do this for him, nor for a thousand like him. For suddenly she had lost all her fear in her instinctive hatred of him. She saw in him now nothing but an unscrupulous implaccable foe, and she was no longer afraid.

When she saw that he had no intention of giving her way she said to him coldly would he allow her to pass. And he said the pass was for everyone, it was as much for his use as for hers.

'You have no business here at all,' she said hotly, 'this is my husband's rent-land and mine. You are trespassing.'

But he only laughed at her, showing his teeth, with scarcely any sound coming from his lips at all.

She said, 'If you don't stand out of my way, you will hear more about this.' And saying this she brushed past him like an angry hen.

He let her go without another word. She was ruffled, and her indignation lasted her until she reached home, and because she could not contain it longer, but must needs share it with someone, she told Ephraim all about meeting the ranger in the pass by their field and having words with him.

Ephraim said, darkly, 'I wonder what he is looking for there?'

And she said with much feeling, she wished to God she knew, but it wasn't going to happen again, she would find a way to put a stop to it. She said Ephraim should go and complain to Busha that his ranger had no business to go snooping around tenants' provision grounds. But Ephraim paid no attention to her words, and her indignation all but boiled over against him, too.

The week hadn't passed before the catastrophe fell upon them. Bananas had been cut from the plantation again, foot tracks were found leading to Ephraim's field, and there amid some high grass almost in the centre of the field they found the stolen fruit hidden. The portions of the stems left on the trees fitted exactly the portions that came away with the bunches.

The news spread over the district like wildfire. Ephraim was the one who was stealing bananas from the plantation. The evidence was completely damning. Ephraim's explanations were unsatisfactory. He was tried in the Resident Magistrate's court and sentenced to serve a prison term for stealing bananas.

Before they took him down to the lock-up he swore to Mabel that he was innocent, and he took a terrible oath that he would not rest until he had paid off the man who had brought this thing upon him.

He actually served only fourteen days in prison, and then he was released. He returned home a still more silent man, and something dark brooded just behind his eyes all the time.

He called in three butchers and sold all his goats, and his cow and calf, and his three pigs, without even consulting Mabel by so much as telling her beforehand what his intentions were. And Mabel, although she looked worried, with lines of age in her face, never questioned him. She just stood aside and let him do as he pleased without so much as a thought of complaint for herself. But somehow all the fire seemed to have gone out of her again, and in its place was that old fear, but now multiplied an hundredfold.

In the weeks that passed Ephraim sold every single thing they had, all to the clothes on their backs, their beds, and the iron cooking-pot in the yard.

And one moonless night Mabel came awake suddenly as though someone had shaken her roughly by the shoulder. She turned over on her side and found that the bed was empty but for herself. Ephraim had gone. In the dead of night he had stolen away from her side. Then the old nausea of fear came over her in great waves, and she lay sleepless, sweating and shivering as one with an ague. She spent the rest of the night praying for Ephraim and herself, and for their happiness together.

But in the morning she rose and cooked breakfast and comforted herself by telling the two little girls that their papa had gone away on some urgent business, but that he would soon be home again.

She waited all that day, and the next in a state of desolation, and on the third day Ephraim returned. But it was the old steady, staunch, easy-going Ephraim come back to her again, the Ephraim she had known before their trouble had come upon them. And although her heart yearned for him to tell her all, yet never by word or gesture once did she press him.

Three days passed, and on the evening of the third day the ranger was reported missing. On the morning of the fourth day they found him dead out in the field, and his body had come to corruption, they were able to identify him only by the clothes he wore. And everybody thought that here indeed was witchcraft, for how else could a man's body come to corruption in a few short hours of the night, for the ranger had been seen in the bar of the Chinaman's shop drinking and playing dominoes until late in the evening. But that night he didn't turn up to take his shotgun from the office and make his round of the plantation, and the very next morning the thing was found out in the field.

But everybody said that whatever had happened it served him right, and no one was sorry that he was dead. And they remembered how Ephraim had raised all that money, and had made a certain journey to an unknown destination in the dead of night and had returned after three days; and again it was on three days, and now this thing befell. But no man spoke his thoughts aloud, from reasons of caution. And everyone was extra respectful of Ephraim ever after that; well, for quite a time anyway.

And then one day a stranger, who laughed and drank and diced a lot, stopped in passing through the district. And he began telling all sorts of tall tales in the rum shop, and among them was a certain tale of wonder that set them all speculating again.

The tale the stranger told was how in his district there was a certain man who had died. He was a bad man, but because of some powerful black magic he gave himself the power to rise again; but because he was afraid that the people of his own district might not like it seeing him whom they knew to be dead alive again in their midst, he had betaken himself to another district far away, in the dead of night. But some boys who were up and about early, catching up their mules which they were pasturing illegally in a field of guinea grass belonging to someone else – an important person, and a Justice of the Peace – had set the rumour current that they had seen him. The rumour became so persistent that some were for having the grave opened to see whether or not the body was still there; but nobody would have anything to do with the actual opening of it. For you see, not only did these boys see the man, but others as well. An old woman who made her living by mixing and selling herbs, and a man coming home drunk from a spree, and the girl who worked at the parsonage, who later had a baby for the blacksmith – all these people saw that miracle, as well.

'That's a funny sort of business,' old Ebenezer Smikle said, shaking his head.

'It's the truth. If you disbelieve me you go to that district and ask anyone. They will tell you.'

'What would a man want to come alive for after he was properly dead? I call that flying in the face of providence,' was the opinion of James Telfer who was a pork butcher and a deacon in the church besides.

'He was a bad man, a very very bad man. He practised obeah and caused the end of many a good man before him.'

'But a man like that now, would he ever die again, proper, and be buried decent like the first time, I wonder?' Obediah Williams asked.

'He wouldn't be really a man at all, but a sort of ghost, I reckon. Only someone with a stronger magic could lay him.'

'Now suppose you was to get this man with the stronger magic to lay him,' said old man Smikle. 'What you think . . .?'

'How you mean?'

'I mean what would happen to his mortal body, his remains?'

At this the stranger laughed hugely, as though it all struck him as something very funny indeed.

'You're askin' me!' he said.

The Miracle

THE water from the gourd had a brackish taste. The woman had taken it up to the spring and filled it again after they had had their midday meal. In spite of its brackishness however, he tilted it up against his chin and drank deeply. The afternoon had been fiercely hot, and he had been working with mechanical precision, without haste, but without stopping to rest.

As he cleared the ground with his machete the woman raked up the bush behind him into heaps. Later, when the sun had dried them, they would set fire to them, and then the field would be ready for digging. He would dig hills for yams and cocoas among the stones that littered this cockpit country like crystals of salt from a giant shaker. The woman would follow behind with a broken machete, making little pockets in the rich, loamy earth, and into each pocket she would drop three red kidney beans, firming them with the pressure of her foot.

He watched her now with eyes that were dull and expressionless, while she gathered a bundle of dry sticks for firewood. She went about this with mechanical, lifeless motions that lacked enthusiasm, and yet she sang in a clear, pure contralto as though giving expression to something deep within her that held all her store of hope, and courage, and inspiration . . . something beyond the dull mechanics of existence, that kept her spirit aware, and the flicker of hope alive and vivid against the medium-grey of her immediate and material outlook.

His own eyes too held no flicker of interest as he regarded her. His was an animal acceptance of things . . . his the routine of the beast of burden. He worked hard all day knowing that it earned him a square meal and a full night's rest. Each day brought its own fulfilment at the end. There was nothing outside of that . . . no promise outside of that, that an aggregate of many days of uninspired, uninterupted toil might fulfil.

He stirred himself from his recumbent position against the dry stump of a tree he had felled months ago.

'Sarah,' he called.

It was the signal for which she waited. It meant that it was time for them to start on their homeward journey. They had a long way to go over a narrow and stony track. Her song ended abruptly, as though, now that it had served her for the hour, she would lay it away in that place where she kept her secret reserves of strength and inspiration.

When the evening meal was over he filled his pipe with shredded rope tobacco which she cut up for him as he needed it. He sat on the doorstep of their little bungalow and smoked in silence, with that dull film settling over his unmoving gaze – as though, looking out into the night, he saw nothing, heard nothing.

Twenty, thirty years ago he had planned ahead for now. This present had been the inspired future then. But what had come of all his planning? At fifty he was doing the same things that he had been doing when he was a young man of twenty or so, and he would go on in just this groove until he died.

If they had had a child, there would have been *that* to work for, to hope for, to plan ahead for. There would be some sense in giving hostages to a future that promised an heir worthy to reap the rewards of all that hoping and travailing. But they had had no child of their union, and now he was past hoping for one . . . there was nothing to do but just carry on in this groove until the end.

It had been brought home to him, not so many years ago, that this was even his destiny, and it was no use struggling against it . . . trying to move out of his rut. It was then that he had decided at last to realise at least one of his ambitions. It had been an act of pure selfishness, but he had been driven to it by the very fear of that bleak and barren outlook. With all hope gone, the loneliness of his declining years would be unbearable.

He had had to grasp at it while there was yet time. And so he had taken a wife who was nearly thirty years younger than he. He had even cherished the hope at first that she might bear him a son, and so change all this – his outlook – tinting it with hope, imbuing him with a new life, a new determination to make good against all odds. But now he knew beyond the shadow of doubt that their union was destined to be a barren one. So he had cheated, and been cheated, even in that. Still he held no sort of grudge against life. He accepted it all dumbly, without any feeling of rebellion against his lot. He was reconciled to life as a slave might be to the whims of his master. He believed in God, and was altogether without bitterness.

She moved about the room with a quiet efficiency, clearing away the remains of their supper . . . washing dishes in a pan of water she had fetched from the spring. When she was finished she came and sat on the step beside him.

She said, without looking at him: 'What are you thinking about?'

He did not reply immediately. She though that perhaps he had not heard her.

'There are so many voices out there, speaking all at once, that you cannot catch a single voice unless you strain your hearing right hard against the tumult of things . . . and yet this is silence as we know it. It is the most stillness that you and I will ever know.''

She was always talking about things like that, in that dreamy, far-away voice of hers, resting her chin upon one hand . . . and yet when it came to working there were few women who could keep up with her. But then she was a true daughter of the soil. Her parents were simple peasant landowners who had saved and scrimped to give her the best education they could afford. She had been a pupil-teacher in a Government school when he had married her. And in spite of his having lost his truck in that accident when it had gone right over a precipice going round a treacherous corner on the Burnt Hill road, filled with people on their way to a distant 'Balm Yard' . . . and in spite of all the bad luck that had dogged him all his days, and the counsel of her friends and her family, she had stuck to him to the last, eventually marrying him. If she ever regretted her choice she never once showed any sign of doing so.

He said suddenly: 'I was not thinking at all, Sarah. I was just looking' on like.'

She rested a hand upon his knee, and the quivering urgency of it told him that she had something on her mind, something that she was excited about. Soon as she could get around to it in her own way, she'd be telling him. But first, he knew, she must prepare the ground. It had always been her way when there was something important she wished to communicate to him.

'Listening to the night is like listening to the ticking of your own thoughts going though the clockworks of your mind, when you're not trying to think. Your thoughts just go ticking on, and on, and presently you begin to be aware of one that seems to have got loose from the rest. It goes on thinking itself over and over like a chipped gramophone record repeating an isolated phrase of a song . . . until you give it a gentle push to help it out of its rut.'

He blurted out something that always seemed to be on his mind. 'A girl who's had your education ought never to have married a man like me. Don't you ever think, Sarah . . . think about things, like what your life might have been if you hadn't been tied to me?'

'Oh, you mustn't say that!' she cried, as if he had hurt her. 'It's not a question of me being tied to you at all. I married you with my eyes wide open to all the facts. I married you because I wanted to – oh, I never would have been as happy with anyone else, I know – I know. There's a lot of things might have been different for us if we'd been able to know beforehand how things would have turned out in the end. But on the whole it hasn't been altogether bad.'

He wanted to say something then, but the pressure of her hand upon his knee suddenly tightened; she hurried on, as though she feared she might be side-tracked from saying what was on her mind.

'We were talking about ruts, weren't we? Well, I've been thinking things over. You know I've got a little money saved up in the post office bank from the sugar we sold last year, after paying off the last instalment on the truck. And I was thinking maybe if you took it out and went to the garage they'd let you have another truck. It isn't much to pay down on a new one, but they know you're honest and hard working. They know how hard you worked to pay them back for the truck that was lost in that accident. And . . .'

But he would not let her go on. 'Stop, Sarah. I can't stand to hear you talk like that. Listen child . . . Talking about ruts, weren't we? Well, for thirty years I've planned and sweated to get out of this one I'm in, trying to make a living off the bit of land left me by my father. I was doing well with it – if I'd only had the sense to know it. I was able to save enough money to lease Mass Jim's twenty acre pasture and plant out ten acres of it in bananas. And then what happened? I started out doing mighty well. At that time a field of well cultivated bananas on good land was good for a net profit of anywhere between ten and twenty pounds per acre, per annum – barring hurricanes. Well, there you have it. After the first year we had hurricanes three years in succession, coming right on top of each other. I came back to my father's land. I worked hard and made it pay. My brother returned from Cuba with a bit of cash. We threw in everything we had, cleared the mortgage, started making a little money again above expenses, and we put it aside in the post office bank until we had enough to make the down payment on the truck. At that time, remember, there was money to be made in trucking bananas from here to Montego Bay, because the railway don't run through these parts, and the Burnt Hill road had just been cut – you could slice off a good piece of the journey going through there. We got up to sixpence per count bunch for truckage. Lots of fellows were cashing in on it. Slim who started scratch with us now owns a fleet of six trucks. He's built himself a fine new home right on top of a hill overlooking the village. And there's that fellow from Halliburton, and the Chinaman from English Hill . . . it would take me the fingers of both my hands to tell them all. But what happened to *us* . . . Well, you know all about that . . . Amos didn't have to work Sundays carrying passengers to balm meetings. I begged him not to. But he said he could get up a dollar a head taking them there and back. Well something happened to the truck going round that corner . . . just what, nobody'll ever know, because Amos was drivin' an' he got killed outright. No Sarah, we're going to save all we can put by so that things will be a little easier for us later on. Don't you know it breaks my heart to see you working so hard, child? And me knowing all the while it's me who's dragged you down to this. If you had . . .'

But she silenced him with her fingers against his lips.

'Hush! Don't ever say that again . . . please. It – pains me to hear you speak like that, Henry.'

The little song that waited upon her lips when the long, hot afternoon hours dragged on, seemed too far down today for her to reach down for it and drag it forth. Although her firm slender body was filling out with almost matronly curves she felt as though her flesh was wasted, and a new and alien weariness settled upon her limbs, and about her spirit too, weighing her down.

It was the heat of the sun, she would go and rest a spell under the shade of that tree where the water gourd hung beside his haversack.

There was that thing she had been trying now for days to tell him, but everytime she had been side-tracked somehow. She wanted to know how he would react to this startling bit of news, and yet she feared. She must find some way to communicate it to him, beautifully, gently . . . all the wonder and mystery of it. She must find some way to communicate to him that simple faith and inspiration of hers that had made this miracle possible.

He had wanted so badly to have a child that now they had ceased altogether to speak of it, because the subject was too painful for him. Yet now that she knew she was going to have a child, it was as though her womb moved with pride . . . and something else, something that transcended all other feelings, thoughts, emotions. If only she could make him see the wonder and beauty of it, and the mystery of it . . . it only she could make him see.

She would be patient with him. She would try to shepherd his mind down those channels of deep inner understanding, that would make him see with her eyes of wholeness, of more than mortal seeing. She would say: 'You must have faith, Henry. If only you would have faith as a grain of mustard seed, all things would be possible . . .' She would make him believe it possible – he *must* be made to believe. For this thing that she had deliberately brought upon herself, she had done out of the wholeness, the wonder and the immaculation of her love for him . . . to awaken within him a new courage, a new confidence . . . to give him life again, and hope again. And in very truth it was a miracle. It was a sacred miracle of miracles . . . it was the miracle of immaculate late conception.

He had asked for a child of her womb and he would have it. She had faith . . . she had the wonderful inspiration and simple faith to take this interpretation of her act to the very core of her consciousness. This immaculation was not earthy – it was of fire, and symbolical. To her it was true, and pure, and simple . . . like the simple act of her faith.

She must make him see it in the light of a miracle . . . The voice of God had spoken to her in the night . . . 'Sarah, arise now, and go here, and do thus . . .' Surely he would believe – even as she believed.

She need not initiate him into the details of it. She would simply tell him that she had prayed, because she knew he desired a child of her . . . and God had answered her prayer.

God had shown her that it was a means to an end – the end being the salvation of him.

After she had made him see all this, she would make him see that it was right and reasonable that he should give up his blind serfdom to the soil and try again. She would make him take the money out of the post office savings bank and make a down payment on a new truck. She would imbue him with her simple and beautiful faith that was just a pure and wonderful act of acceptance.

He saw tht she rested under the shade of a tree, and so he went himself and gathered the firewood for their evening meal.

After supper she cut up the rope tobacco into shreds, rolling it between her hands and filling his pipe for him.

He removed the pipe from his mouth, and patted the crown of her head.

'There, there,' he said soothingly. 'You always get them fancy ideas into your little head when you're too tired for anything else. Better take it easy, Sarah. Don't want to have you get sick on my hands. I guess it would be just about the last straw. Of course I believe in God, but I don't believe in no bloomin' miracles, like them Balm of Gilead people do. No Ma'am!'

She looked up at him then, her features drawn into the thin lines of intentness. She trembled a little with the fierce energy of conviction. 'But this is a *real* miracle, Henry.' She looked away. 'I asked God for a miracle, and He gave it to me – don't you see?' she finished, simply.

'Of course, of course, honey. I'm not trying to take away your belief in God. I know you've always been a religious girl. I want for you to stay that way. You know it.'

She roused herself now. She pounded away at his chest with her clenched fists, as though she were trying to batter down the walls of his unbelief.

'Don't try to treat me like a child,' she flung at him fiercely. 'You've got to take me seriously, you hear? You've *got* to believe me! Oh, if you only had a grain of faith you would believe. How could you be so – so cruel after all I've done.'

Her sobs shook him at last out of his complacence.

'What is it, honey?' he asked gently, taking her head upon his shoulder, and stroking her hot cheek tenderly.'

'I – I can't . . . I can't tell you. You wouldn't believe. I know you wouldn't believe me. Oh God! What can I do? I'll kill myself.'

He said sternly, taking her face between his hands, and compelling her eyes with his steadfast, searching gaze: 'What is it? What have you done? Tell me this minute, Sarah. You know there are no secrets between us.'

She shook her head, her eyes glassy with tears.

'No, no. There are no secrets between us. There can never be, Henry. I'm going to have a baby.'

He walked away slowly, fumbling on the step beside him for his pipe. Having found it he put it between his teeth again. Then he took it out and stared at it a long time without saying anything.

His silence terrified her. She wanted to tell him all – to try to communicate to him something of her own feeling about the matter – her whole and beautiful acceptance of it . . . something of the beautiful faith that had inspired her – but she found no words. She bit into the knuckles of her clenched fist and was dumb.

He rose now, ponderously. 'I'm going for a walk,' he announced in a hollow voice, without looking at her.

She lay on the bed quivering with fear of the consequences of her act. She had dragged the bedclothes around her, as though with them she would hold off the evil that menaced her.

Had she done wrong? Now she was in the terrible grip of doubt, uncertainty. 'Oh, God,' she prayed, 'if I have done wrong, let me know now . . . before it is too late . . . before he comes back.'

She thought of the half bottle of Lysol on the shelf above the wash stand . . . 'Oh God, speak to me and tell me if I have sinned. Before it is too late . . . before he returns.'

She had prayed for a miracle, and now she lay on the bed, wide-eyed, unmoving, unthinking, waiting for it to happen.

When he came in the lamp was burning on the table. There was something in this room now that affected him powerfully . . . something like a presence that he could feel without seeing . . . something outside of the three dimensions of physical perception, yet real and conclusive – like the lamp on the table – for all that.

She lay on the bed unmoving. She might have been dead for all the indications she gave to the contrary. The taste of the pipe was rank and acid upon his tongue. He had forgotten to light it. Outside there he had forgotten his physical surroundings, it was as though all that was substantial had fallen away from him, leaving his thoughts – or rather, the single thought – like a raw, quivering nerve surrounded by insensate matter that for the time had ceased to exist. Then slowly the dumb unquestioning acceptance of this too had been forced upon him. He assimilated it slowly, painfully at first, until it became a part of that brute stoicism that was his.

He was trembling violently, like a leaf in the wind.

She lay there seemly so peaceful so assured – it was not complacence; she was anchored upon something that was beyond him. What was it about her that had the power to confirm and ratify her act absolutely, within her own mind? It baffled him, made him afraid of her, now that his was past. He felt so small, so futile and defenseless before it . . .

He went over to the bed and took her gently in his arms. His face searched hers as though asking for a sign . . . some assurance upon which to establish that within him that reached out blindly for recognition, articulation. That was it, he wanted some of her strength and assurance from her, to stay him.

Her head fell limply against his shoulder. She was muttering thickly, like a child overcome with sleep.

'I thought I was brave . . . but now I know I am afraid . . . Forgive me, Henry.'

'Sarah, honey!' he said. 'Sarah!' holding her fiercely to him.

But inside here, with her lying upon the bed, with nothing articulate but the lamp burning on the table, something had been revealed to him in a flash . . . something that was so much outside of his experience that for the instant it left him stunned, awed in its presence. It was a revelation that came and went like the opening and shutting of a blade of lightning in the sky of night. Almost before he was aware of it, it was gone. And yet it seemed to open up now potentialities of understanding with his mind . . . so that he was left floundering on the brink of his accustomed darkness, and was now oppressively aware of it as such. Where he had been conscious of nothing before, he saw now a negative blackness in his mind, a gape of emptiness, an absence of light. He was shaken, afraid . . . he knew that urgency of being that is focused at a single white point of intensity . . . the desire to see again as he had, almost unconsciously in that vivid revealing flash, with eyes that were of more than mortal seeing . . . to stand bathed completely in that light again, to feel the comfort and warmth and poignancy of it, and the sustaining wholeness and presence of it.

Flood Water

THE river ran all the way through his field, dividing it in two. Today it ran flush to the grass on either bank with yellow water that was treacherous because it gave little indication of the force of the current beneath; treacherous like a woman who is all body, and bad. But usually the river was clear and swift and robust, dimpling over the rapids, and blue and cool and clear to the sandy bottom below the fording. Like a woman who has no secrets from the world, and is virgin in her mind and without deceit. But it had been raining off and on for the past three days, and higher up in the hills again where there were a hundred little streams that fed the river, it was raining worse. That made the difference.

He took off his boots at the fording and waded across with water up to his knees, part of the way.

The old man, 'Lijah, who had the field adjoining his was there before him today.

'Boy Peters,' he said. They called him Boy. That was his name. Although he was a tall strapping fellow in his early twenties. 'Boy Peters, boy,' old 'Lijah greeted, 'H'm. Goin' be trouble wid de old woman if it keep on rainin'.'

He knew the old fellow was speaking of the river. They always did in those terms. They both had fields that lay across the river, and times past they had had to outwit her, or best her in some manner, in order to get to their fields and back. Twice before the fording had been washed away altogether. Once he had swam the muddy treacherous stretch of water to get across to the other bank before nightfall. That was on account of Bella. Before she had come to live with him, sharing his home with him as man and wife. He would do it again, because he couldn't bear to be away from her, spending all of a whole night in a cold damp hut on the side of the hill with only the old man for company.

The old man thought he was a fool for risking his life. But he could afford to laugh at him, knowing his own strength, that he could always best that old river in a test of cunning or sheer brute force. Swim with the current downstream, that was it, and all the time fight your way out and across to the other side. But all you do don't let her pull you under.

'You're a fool, Boy Peters. Once you win, not to say you win all the time. Some day she goin' to pull you under,' he had said, and it was as though he was terribly anxious for the boy the way he said it. It was plain the old man loved him like a son.

So now, 'Boy Peters, boy, goin' be trouble wid de old woman if it keep on rainin' like this up in de hills,' he said. Thinking in the back of his canny old head that maybe it *was* going to keep on raining like this all day, up there in the hills.

Peters laughed and chopped a green stick in two with his machete in one stroke, so that the lower portion of it whistled away into the bushes as though he had flung it from him with all his might.

'Don't mean nothin' to me no matter what she do. Ain't nothin' I'm askin' of her in the way of favours, old man. I just figure to take what I want, and to get across before nightfall is the thing I fancy.'

The old man said nothing, and for some obscure reason this displeased the other. Perhaps he wanted to argue with the old man, to brag a bit about how young and strong he wasy, with the cruelty of youth in its disdain of age. But the old man said nothing. Maybe he was thinking how it would be with this boy one day, old too, and knowing a powerful lot more than he did today. If he lived long enough.

There was something of dignity, and of melancholy too in the untroubled face of old 'Lijah, standing there sucking at the pipe in the act of lighting up.

'I been a young man like you meself,' he said, presently, looking steadily at the other. 'Don't forget that, Boy Peters. I seen plenty things in my life. An' I learn two things I'll never forget to the longest day I live. One of them is you never know what's going on inside a woman's mind, an' the other is that that old debbil-river is more full of contrariness an' cunning than any woman.'

He settled his knapsack on his hip and sat down on a tree stump, still holding the glowing coal to his pipe. It seemed to the younger man that, in his greater age and perhaps his greater knowledge of life, the old man stood apart in the sense of inaccessibility, and he was conscious of irritation. What had he to say that he didn't know? What dark knowing lived within that almost senile brain? It was preposterous. And yet . . . something about the old fellow's undeliberated aloofness made him uncomfortable in a way that was a little frightening. Thinking about what he had said about women. Thinking about Bella. Not taking so much from the words themselves, but something in his way of saying them. Deep, deep as hell. The trouble with people when they are getting old. Couldn't have been thinking of meaning Bella, though; the old cuss.

It had been raining up in the hills all right. All afternoon. You could tell that by the way the sun was doused in mist, and the way the thunder of the river grew and grew in the distance. But he didn't care. He wasn't even thinking about it, much. What he was thinking of now was getting on back home. And across the river. To Bella. Home. He knew all about her cunning. He would always come out besting her knowing what he knew. Across the muddy treacherous water and Bella, warmth and a fire; hot food, home.

The old man said, standing in the middle of the pass, looking at him. 'Now you ain't goin' to do nothin' foolish I hope, Boy Peters. I got the hut all fixed an' ready. Plenty of dry grass to keep you warm outside.' He slapped the knapsack on his hip. 'An plenty of good grub, an' rum to warm you inside.'

It might have been he hadn't heard him.

'Bella,' he said, slowly his eyes never leaving his face. 'Bella won't be expectin' you, neither.'

He almost brushed him aside he was so angry; without any reason that he could tell himself. Angry inside him because of something about the old man that was dark with angry foreboding and ugly too. He saw him now with venom. Something about a rumour in the village that he hadn't listened to anyway. Something to do with Bella. He could see it now. Almost he was on the point of striking him down. Only just caught himself up in time, remembering there wasn't anything the old man had actually said. Must be it was in him though, inside him. He could feel it. And it was a damned lie. Just to show him he would swim that river. And then he would sit on a rock on the other side and laugh at him, at his age and impotence. Just to show him.

He stood beside the muddy water in its mad race downstream, stood stripped to the waist, muscled like a bronze god, and rippling with latent strength.

Plunge in, and swim with the current, but cutting across it diagonally all the time, until you were out of it, on the other side. That was it. As easy as that. But always mind she don't pull you under.

The water took him in the first moment of impact and rolled him over and over like a log. Half of the time his head was under. But always he was fighting, fighting to keep coming up. Something sucked at his legs almost turning him straight across to the full force of the current, but he kicked free – and went under. Rolled over, and went under. There was a roaring noise inside his head. His lungs felt as though they were bursting. But always, even unconsciously, he was fighting, fighting to keep coming up.

He had forgotten about the old man silently watching the unequal struggle from the bank. Forgotten about Bella. Something about something somebody said . . .

The roar of the rapids. The thunder of death in his ears. He would be broken to ribbons on the rapids. The rocks. His skull smashed in. His limbs all but torn from his body. He was fighting like a hundred demons, fighting blind with the roar of the rapids in his ears, and above him a million tons of water like blood weighing him down.

And then he was out of the current, and across . . . Something about something someone had said about a river, and what would happen if it sucked you under . . . He couldn't tell if he lived to be a thousand years how it happened. He had just managed, was all he knew. He hadn't done it himself, either. It just happened as though he had been shot out of a gun. And there he was kicking free and near dead. But on the other side. Out of the current. He had got across.

He pulled himself weakly up on to the bank with the aid of some tree roots. And then his strength left him and he just lay in the grass and breathed with painful gasps.

He may have lain there for hours. It was getting dark. Someone was shouting from across the river. He suddenly remembered the old man. They were like father and son.

He pulled himself up at last to a sitting posture, leaning his back against a stone. He wanted to shout back, across the gathering darkness. To make him know he had got across; that he was safe. But first he must catch his breath. He still felt strangely weak.

One thing though he would never boast about being able to best the old river, never again. She had had him licked. She had all but done for him back there. A miracle had saved him alive and brought him to the other side.

He stood up now and waved his arms and shouted. Shouted to the man who was as his father, standing anxiously on the other side. A strange delirium seemed to take possession of him at once. He was across and alive. A miracle had happened. He shouted and waved his arms. Wanting the old man to know he was safe, on the other side, and not somewhere inside the belly of the river.

He wanted to hug the old man to him, and lift him up in his arms, and prance with him all over the grass, he was so happy to have come across, and to be alive and whole, and not dead without the meaning of life, somewhere in the belly of the river.

Presently the shouting died down from the opposite bank. And now there only remained the steady, tremendous roar of the demon river. And darkness came down and found him standing there alone, and chill to the marrow.

He turned and went slowly up the narrow pass – to home, the warmth of a fire, and the woman he loved, preferring death to the thought that he might share her with another.

A Tree Falls

HE LAID aside the axe, and the waves of silence that had parted before him as he made his careless way to the heart of the forest, flowed back as with a sigh. The silence flattened itself out over the entire vast valley, clothing the rocks and the trees, thick and palpable like the river mist – hiding at its patient core the certain knowledge that even the axe with its rude foreign exclamations, venturing there with the brave clamour that cloaks fear, foretold its own stammering, inevitable surrender.

It seemed to him that he heard stealthy footsteps somewhere behind him . . . the snapping of dried twigs . . . the leafy whisper of green ones, as invisible fingers put them aside to allow unhindered the passage of the ghostly inhabitants of the wilderness.

He made no attempt to turn his head, because he knew he would see no one . . . and ever the silence would settle back with the passing of these tiny ripples of sound that ringed its smooth surface . . .

Again the axe sang its victorious note against the thin, vibrating walls that took it and threw it backward and forward, multiplying it a thousand times.

Fresh chips from the great tree spattered the coffee-brown of its rotted leaves of centuries . . . It creaks throughout its mighty girth . . . It teeters – or so it seems – with the thrust of the wind through its boughs that have reached during its lifetime ever triumphantly upward, until they tower a hundred feet in the air.

It is leaning a little now . . . it yearns over the valley that has known it these hundred years, where it has spread the tallest shadow, and wove the silence within its leaves and branches, like the shuttles of a tremendous loom, spinning away the close fabric of tremendous and unending twilight that might shadow the heart of the stoutest with unreasoning terror.

The man is exultant. The wound in the tree's side has laid bare the great red heart of mahogany. In this tree there is a small fortune for the taking. There is not another tree like it in all the length and breadth of these virgin wooded Crown lands.

The men with the saws are in the hills beyond, keeping a watchful lookout for the Crown Forest-Rangers – for the thunder of his axe travels far in this wilderness. If a Ranger should appear they will make the smoke-signal, while ostensibly roasting wild Imba-roots over a fire. They will, if necessary, keep the Ranger there, swapping stories with him, allowing him to fill his pipe from their supply of tobacco, offering him roasted Imba-root and jerked pork on the end of a sharpened stick.

He is alone in the valley with this giant that is slowly bowing to his relentless axe.

He is forced to pause again to rest and catch his breath . . . the giant is tougher even than he thought. Stubbornly the great axe stands, resisting valiantly to the last the terrible assaults of the axe.

He is tired . . . he leans heavily against the handle of his axe, the blade of which is buried so deep into the solid heart of the tree, that his full weight upon it will not shake the axe.

Silence fills the valley again. Ghostly whispers of silence . . . the snapping of dried twigs, now here, now there . . . the sibilant query and protest of leaves in the underbrush that part to let the ghostly ones pass . . . then the ripples on the face of silence are smoothed over, as it settles back again, calm and enigmatic like the face of a pool, or a poker-player.

He is a brave man, not easily frightened. He is inured to the menace of the wilderness, its silence. Yet strange sensations tingle down his sweating spine. Strange thoughts thrust aside the one that was uppermost in his mind . . . the gloating triumph of the moment.

And then they turned to home and the woman who waited his coming – herself a tree – a sapling tree heavy with the promise of fruitage.

There would be a great round pan of corn-pone in the kitchen, cold, when he got back . . . and a woman's arms about him – his woman.

The extension he was adding to their home would need some hardwood joists and beams, and cedar shingles for the roof. He would use only the finest native lumber, as usual. The finest native lumber to be had in these parts came from off the vast wooden tracts of virgin Crown lands. It was his for the taking, if only he could out-smart the Government Rangers and Bailiffs.

In the out-shed, hidden away under the bundle of shavings, was the wooden axe he was carving as a gift for the son that would be his. It just had to be a boy, because he didn't have any use for girl children. What in the world would he do with her? His boy now, would become a lumber-man like himself, like his father was before him. He would teach him all the tricks of the trade . . . He would be well equipped to carry on the traditions of the family, and grow up to be a prosperous and respected citizen.

There would be a thick slab of corn-pone in the kitchen on his return . . .

Again the strange thoughts – unnamed fears, premonitions . . . the quick snapping of twigs . . . a sudden scurry of fallen leaves along the forest floor . . . overhead the giant tree trembled and groaned in its agony . . .

His eyes went suddenly to the crest of the furthest hill.

Was that the signal of his men? He put a hand to his forehead and peered out from beneath it. No, it was only a wisp of cloud, like a ghostly, nebulous, writhing axe . . . an axe imbedded in the heart of a great tree of cloud. For a moment it seemed to him menacing with omen.

He laughed at his own fears, and was immediately shocked and abashed by the profound, pained silence that followed it. Strange that the valley did not echo his laughter. He laughed again – louder and longer this time – then cupped his hand to his ear, leaning forward, every nerve strained, listening. From far down the valley came a thin whisper of derisive echoes.

He put his head back defiantly and opened his mouth to laugh again, distending his bellows-like lungs to their fullest . . . and suddenly changed his mind.

He knocked with the heel of his hand sharply against the handle of the axe, several times, to make it loosen its death grip upon the tree. Then he swung it aloft again.

He could hear the ringing, exultant echoes of the axe, though . . . the mean silence of the valley dared not withhold that sound! The triumphant, gloating laughter of the axe split that silence in two again, throwing it back upon itself in great twin waves that towered higher than the mountains themselves. Very well then, they would heed the sound of his axe and tremble! His heart filled to bursting with pride. He added his own rhythmic grunt at the end of each stroke, to the voice of the axe.

The great tree-trunk that had mocked the strength of his arm, and the silence that had mocked his puny laughter . . . they belonged to the stubborn reluctance of the unyielding wilderness, his ancient antagonist. But he would show them who was conqueror here, wilderness or man . . . heart of tree, or blade of axe . . .

He would show them . . . *show* them . . . *show* them . . .!

Was that the sound of the giant timber yielding, the great heart of wood breaking at last . . .? or was it just another trick of the wilderness, trying to fool him again, trying to delay the ultimate conquest of his strong arm and his sharp axe-blade over insensate timber? He would show them . . . *show* them . . . *show* them! Each stroke of the axe seemed to bite deeper, deeper. The chips flew in a shower round him . . . red chips now . . . chips from the unyielding red heart of mahogany! . . .

Without further warning the great tree suddenly bowed, seemed to hesitate an instant, suspended at an impossible slant, yet reluctant to the last, battling against the inevitable to the last. Then with a mighty roar it thundered to the ground. The trunk leaped in the air, gave a spasmodic sideways kick as the tough branches a hundred feet away, hit the first obstacle of rock. Then it reared high up again, as though it would complete a somersault, and crashed to its side, lying with the angle of the valley.

A flight of winged reverberations took the air sharply, with a mighty thrust of wings – for an instant only – then came quietly to rest again among the branches of the trees and upon the naked spurs of rock. And the waves of silence flowed forward over the valley, covering everything, healing the terrible instant of thunder that had gashed it across.

He had heard the last unmistakable crackle of the falling tree. He had barely time to leap aside, leaving his axe there, sunk in its heart. He saw the lower end rear up into the air, and his heart was almost humbled for a moment. He had sent yet another giant thundering to his doom . . . and almost in the same instant his heart knew terror as he saw the quick sideways kick of the jagged base, spurred and weighted with death. He had no time to avoid it . . . an instant of triumph . . . a split instant of panic . . . and then – nothing . . .

Dusk was settling down over the valley when the sawyers came. They saw the place where the mighty tree had fallen. They shouted their joy and quickened their pace, until they came to the spot where *his* broken body lay.

They stood with bared heads, and tight lips, staring at him. The silence . . . the snapping of dried twigs . . . the ghostly whispers of leaves . . . all these daunted them . . .

They left him where he lay within that vast, that weirdly peopled sepulchre of silence.

Glory Road

THAT Sunday the parson had preached a sermon about thanksgiving. Jeremiah and Lucas had never given much thought to this matter before, and of the three men who were engaged in road cleaning, by 'task-work', the rather morose young man, who was practically a stranger to the district had, until then, given it perhaps the least thought of all. Jake was not his real name, but that was what the other two decided to call him, since a man must have a name by which other men might address him.

Oddly enough it was the normally silent, morose Jake who started the game. They had been discussing the parson's sermon during the lunch hour, as they rested under the shade of a generous guango tree, in the heat of the noon. It was decided that each was to go home that night and observe for himself some particular blessing for which he ought to be thankful. The next day they were each to tell of it.

So Jeremiah went home to his wife, and the first thing with which Matilda met him was the news that their eldest daughter had won a scholarship which would admit her free for three years to a public school for girls. And by way of a mild celebration she had killed a chicken, and had curried it for supper. She knew he was specially fond of curried chicken. Jeremiah was pleased with his daughter's success, of course. He gave her a shilling, and after supper, went out and bought himself a big-gill of rum.

When Lucas got home he found Sarah out. Sarah was not really his wife – but practically that. She came home later. He wanted to know where she had been and what she had done. He had his own private suspicions, which in no wise concern us. The upshot of the ensuing argument was that Lucas beat up his sweetheart again to the high entertainment of the neighbours, and he went to bed drunk, and without any supper.

The first thing Jake did when he got home to the house of the elderly woman who looked after him – got him breakfast and supper, and washed his clothes – was to have a bath. He dried himself with a towel little larger than a man's handkerchief, with 'LAVATORY' marked in red letters all the way across it. He had to stop and wring the towel dry every now and then, so it could do its job of drying him. He stretched his nude limbs and flexed his powerful muscles. He ran his hands down his thighs and legs, let them linger over his shoulders, arms, chest. He did it as though he wanted to make sure of himself. He was a man. Yes, a black man – strong as an ox. A strong man to work and make love to some virile black girl with high, full breasts, and strong, smooth thighs. He was a strong man to fight, too, if need be . . .

A gramophone next door was playing 'The Glory Road', as sung by a famous coloured baritone . . . *'I'm gonna pack my load upon that Glory Road – Glory Road – Glory Road . . .'* The words impinged themselves against his consciousness. He stretched his arms wide and tensed his muscles.

When he dressed himself he was aware of hunger. Yes, he was a strong man to eat a hearty meal, too. He went to a steaming supper of the things he liked best. This old woman certainly did her best to please him. He paid her well. He was no great hand at saving. He liked to live heartily.

When he was finished supper and the things were cleared away, he sent the old woman's little grand-nephew to buy a pint of 'Black Seal' rum. He divided it with the old woman, and swallowed his portion at a single drink. The old crone looked at him wonderingly, admiringly. She longed to talk. She was naturally garrulous. But Jake was no hand at words. He said he would go for a walk. He got easily and comfortably to his feet, pulled out his pipe and started filling it as he sauntered down the little path to the gate.

A couple of hours later he returned. He pulled off his boots and lay on the bed. He was tired and fell asleep quickly . . . And he dreamed a dream . . .

The next morning Jeremiah was eager to begin his account of the previous evening's blessings. The other two could see his eagerness, so they unanimously voted that he should start. Jeremiah rubbing his hands together became positively fervent in his praise of the Lord for the good things He had sent him last night. He dilated upon the curried chicken. It was done just the way he liked it. It was too hot for the pick'neys to eat much of it. Jeremiah said it as though this was in itself a paramount blessing. He was so pleased with the meal that he felt he had to say 'grace' twice – once before, and once after.

As an afterthought he mentioned the reason for the curried chicken – his daughter's scholarship.

As Lucas listened to Jeremiah's account, envy burned within him. But he was determined not to be outdone by the other. So he told a wonderful tale, that for sheer impromptu story-telling would have taken the first prize for a convention of the world's greatest liars. The details of it do not conern this story in any way.

And then it came Jake's turn to tell what he had to be thankful about. He remained silent for a long time, pulling at his pipe, leaning back on the stump of a tree with his eyes closed. They thought he was asleep, but when they voiced this thought aloud his eyes snapped wide open. It seemed as though he was not looking at them so much as through them, and beyond them – way up the road and beyond the last end of it, and beyond the ends of all the roads with which it was joined, or by which it was intersected.

When he spoke they noticed for the first time that he did so without a trace of dialect – almost like an educated man – only this was impossible, because educated men worked in offices and stores, and places where a man could wear clean clothes and appear respectable.

'What have I got to be thankful for?' he said. 'You want me to tell you that. Well, it all came to me in a dream last night. If you wish I will tell you the dream. I dreamt that someone was pointing me down a long road – the longest road in the world. He said: "Jake do you see that road? If you clean a chain of it, you will receive one shilling and sixpence. And when you have cleaned twenty chains of it you will receive thirty shillings. You are a strong man, and you ought to be able to clean twenty chains of road in a working week. As you can see for yourself, it is the longest road in the world, it is so long that if you should live long enough to get to the end of it, you could start all over again from the beginning and never be done cleaning it. And when you are dead, other men will come after you and carry on where you left off.'' And the voice said to me, after a little pause like: "So what, Jake?" And then I got awake.'

The other two were a little nonplussed by this. They did not know what to make of it. They pressed him to interpret it for them. He smiled at them a little tolerantly, a little wearily: 'Look, Jeremiah; look, Lucas, the thing I have to be most thankful for hasn't happened yet. Remember what the man in my dream said: "If you clean twenty chains of road in a working week you will earn thirty shillings." Well, suppose I clean twenty chains, or even thirty chains of road, for so many weeks as it would take me to make enough money to buy myself a big closed car, and a long black cigar, with sixpence left over in my pocket, the happiest thing in life that could happen to me would be to drive down this road in my big car, smoking my long cigar, and come upon the two of you cleaning this road – and stop and give you sixpence to buy yourselves a drink.'

He said this, and started to laugh.

He laughed so loud, and for so long that they were frightened, thinking the sun had touched him. They moved away from him. And when he had stopped laughing the other two went back to work, and the man called Jake went back to lying against the tree stump, and pulling at his pipe, with eyes closed . . .

It was quite dark when he came to himself. The other two had gone home a long time ago. He did not know how late it was. He only knew he must start walking . . . walking as quickly as he could, to get to the furthest place he could from here – and beyond that. Because there was no turning back for him. Maybe there was some meaning to things Beyond . . . beyond *what*? – what was the meaning of this Beyond, anyway? The word had a familiar sound. It used to mean something once, but he had forgotten what.

He kept on walking. He knew not for how long. When he fell down from sheer exhaustion he got up to his feet again with a sob. He was conscious only of two things: that there was never any turning back for him, and that he must not stop walking . . . everything else was like the phenomena of a dream.

Again and again he stumbled and fell. The last time it seemed an eternity before he could gather sufficient strength to get him on his feet again. But he managed to somehow. He could not see where he was going now, but that did not matter either. Only two things made sense: that he mustn't turn back, and that he mustn't stop!

And then he heard the sound of the roar of waters. It was a glad sound. Dimly he was aware that it meant he had got to the end . . . and that meant he would soon be standing on the brink of Beyond . . . that Beyond that scarcely held any meaning for him now, except that in some obscure way it meant . . . he tried to grasp the thought but it evaded him. It was like playing hide-and-seek with oneself. He wanted to laugh, but he was too weary to do that.

The mighty sound of water was nearer now . . . Now it was at his very feet.

A blacker blackness loomed immediately before and beneath him. But he kept right on walking . . .

Part VI

For Ever and Ever

T HE BOY never knew just how or when it happened, but at some stage of their acquaintanceship he realized that he had fallen hopelessly in love. And although for a time it was never spoken of between them, it was there nonetheless, and it seemed to fill all the cirumference of their consciousness.

Gradually from seeing her once a week, over the weekend, his visits became more and more frequent, until it was twice and then three times a week he was seeing her. And now he was at the house every night. They never went out except once a week to see a movie, and occasionally to a night club together. Most of their evenings were spent on the verandah at her home where she lived with relatives, or going for walks. Soon after the gasoline rationing started he was fortunate enough to have got a purchaser for his car. For a time neither of them missed it very much, for they were never much given to gadding about, in search of excitement.

On the north verandah there was a daybed that was used as a couch, and they would spend most of their evenings there, talking about one thing or another, and eating chocolates or grapes, which he brought her frequently.

It was Etta, who was by far the more practical of the two, who put into words the thought that for a long time had been in the minds of them both. It was there all along in his, of course, but somehow it seemed to him unnecessary to talk about anything like that; taking the present always as sufficient unto itself.

It happened the night when he first became aware of that spirit of moodiness that seemed periodically to take possession of her, that spirit that manifested itself in a restlessness that at times could be frightening.

138

But this was really the first time that he had become aware of it as an integral part of herself, of that personality which was and had always been a mystery to him.

Tonight she shrank away from his touch; and he just sat there watching her with his hurt in his eyes.

'Oh, what's the use,' she said.

He saw that the shoulder nearest him twitched with a sudden passionate movement.

She turned toward him suddenly with that impulsiveness that set his blood racing.

'I'm not the girl for you, Joe. There, you may as well know it. You think I am good, but I am not. I am not the least bit good. I want life – I want to do things. There!'

'Etta, what's come over you?' he said with a kind of hopeless agony in his voice that laid bare all his suffering.

'Nothing's come over me. I'm just being myself, that's all. I am tired of all this sham. I just can't go on any longer without facing up to myself, the self that I know I am, that's all.'

And now he saw that there were tears in her eyes. Real tears. There was nothing sham about them.

He reached out a hand and touched her shoulder gently. She turned with a little cry and hid her face against his coat.

'There,' he said, awkwardly. 'Don't be upset. Tell me what is wrong.'

'Oh, Joe dear. Dear dear Joe. It is nothing at all. It is only me being a wretched little fool, that's all.'

But suddenly the thing that would mend all this, that would set all things right, once and for all, dawned upon him with the impact of a great revelation and a great resolve.

'When shall we get married?' he said.

And then she started to laugh.

'Forgive me, Joe. I didn't mean to.'

'It's all right, old girl. It's come as a bit of a shock to you; the way it came to me, just now. But as you say, we've got to face it.'

'Oh, Joe. You're too, too wonderful. You're a darling,' she said, pressing herself to him.

But somehow she avoided the direct reference to marriage

between them after that night. And whenever that spirit of moodiness returned to threaten their happiness, he would take her in his arms like a little child, and soothe and comfort her.

And then one night this thing, whatever it was, seemed to take overmastering possession of them, swept them off their feet altogether and made them aware of its terrible power to put everything asunder, denying everything but its own terrible will.

After this, Joe reasoned within himself, they would have to get married. And it didn't matter a rap whether or not they could afford it. Others had got married on less than he earned. They would just have to manage somehow, and that was all. Nothing now could alter or hinder that.

But still she seemed uncertain in her own mind. It was not that she really cared for money and the things that money could buy, in the sense of being a greedy little bitch. But there was something about the starkness and insecurity of a life of poverty that frightened her. Her parents had been very poor. She had seen all her life how it made their lives bare and bitter and hard, without any touch of beauty or tenderness to redeem it, and it frightened her.

And when he began to press her, she found that the immediate remedy for his impatience lay within herself; and in this way she kept him outwardly contented and well in hand, and off the dangerous ground of what the future held for them. For already she had learned that in his rather simple way he was apt to surrender all in the all-sufficiency of the present, letting well alone.

But all the same, despite all her efforts to evade the issue, it was there. Real. Ever-present; something they had to face. As the weeks went by he became more thoughtful. His face lost something of its extreme youthfulness, and took on certain hard little lines about the mouth, and became somewhat drawn and sullen.

'I am tired of this hole-in-the-corner business,' he said abruptly one night. 'We can't go on like this forever.'

'You mean,' she said, snuggling up closer to him, 'your love won't last forever? Its something to think about.'

She said it half-jokingly. But he was not in the mood for bantering.

'You know I don't mean that,' he said. 'You know perfectly well what I mean.'

She was silent for a time, not knowing what to say. She had said it all before. And it only hurt him unnecessarily to go on repeating the same things. And then she had a sudden inspiration.

'I know what it is, Joe. We're getting tired of doing the same things, night after night. I was reading a book the other day. It said that if you want to get out of a rut, just to go out and do something different. Anything, do your hair in a new style. Go and visit someone you haven't seen for years. Go for a holiday to some place you have never been before. Break the chain of old habits, and start an entirely new chain of causes in motion.'

'Yes,' he said, but without much enthusiasm.

'Well, for a long time, in fact ever since the gasoline shortage, I have wanted to get a bicycle and learn to ride it. You'll teach me, Joe. Won't you? Then we could go for long rides together. Do all sorts of wonderful new things together. Think, Joe, what fun it will be.'

The idea appealed to him immediately. Certainly this was not just a silly superstition about setting in motion a chain of new causes; all that stuff. Here was something eminently practical, something after his own fashion of thinking. A wonder he hadn't thought of it himself.

So they got the bicycle, and Joe started teaching her to ride. Himself, he had been riding a bicycle ever since he had sold his car, of course.

She learned very quickly. So much so that after about the first week he would call for her only to find that she had gone out riding by herself.

The first time it happened he went straight home, because he was tired, and not altogether sorry that he would have the evening to himself. Surprisingly enough he found that it was a pleasant relief to take an evening off every once in a while. There was something to be said for that. Trust Etta to think of it first.

But when she started going off alone like that, and returning quite late, with noticeable regularity, until now it was happening twice a week, he began to be a little resentful of it. It seemed to him that she had started a chain of new causes with a vengeance. Or rather the bicycle had done that for her. But all the same her moodiness and restlessness had entirely passed. That much was to the good.

They had one or two slight tiffs about her going off on her own like that every Wednesday and Friday evening, but nothing much. It was not until it happened that one Thursday evening he turned up to find that she had gone out again, that he really seemed put out.

She told him that she had gone to visit a girl friend of hers about some dress patterns that she had promised to lend her. But he still showed his resentment. There was a sort of slow anger that burned within him, that she had noticed only of late. And in a way it disturbed and frightened her.

'You could have got word to me, at least, and saved me making a fool of myself coming here,' he said.

'Please don't let us quarrel, Joe. I am sorry, and I have said so already. Come on in and forget about it, can't you. How's everything?'

'You were out Wednesday night, too. If you want me to stop coming to see you, if you're tired of me, why don't you say so.'

She looked at him steadily for a long time, without saying anything.

Presently: 'Aren't you coming in, then?' she said.

He went slowly up the steps without looking at her.

But the very next night she got him on the 'phone early. Would he come up and go riding with her to Rockfort? It was Friday night and he had planned to go to a friend's house to play bridge. All right, he said, he would cancel his appointment and come right over. The chaps would have to manage without him somehow.

They sat on the beach and watched the moon come up over the old fort wall. They climbed up to the top of the escarpment and looked out to sea.

'Somehow everything seems to be different,' said Joe, presently. He was troubled, though he could not put his finger on the thing that troubled him. 'This taking so many nights off every week from seeing each other is getting to have too much importance, it seems to me; its getting to be almost as important as seeing each other, don't you think?'

'Please,' she said, putting a hand up to his shoulder, but without withdrawing her gaze from the expanse of water rippling in the moonlight all below them. 'Please,' she said, 'let's not talk just now. Let's just be satisfied with all this for the moment. After that, if you wish to talk – if there is anything to talk about . . .'

And because there was nothing for it but that he fell in with her mood, albeit a little sullenly.

He never asked her where she went or what she did on the evenings she chose to go riding alone. Never once did it enter into his mind that he should ask her. It was just to him that they had these evenings free to themselves to do with as they wished. She never asked him where he went or what he did, and in the same way he never thought to ask her.

But one night by a curious coincidence he came upon her unexpectedly. She was riding with a man he did not know. He was much older than she was, and he had an air about him of comfortable proprietorship that came quite natural to him. You could see at a glance what sort of man he was; a personality. A man of culture, and all that goes to make for that thing known as background. He had it all, and he was probably wealthy on top of that. And besides he could have been her father.

They had not seen him because he was behind them. And he had no intention of overtaking them and being seen. He kept a good distance between them all the way down the Halfway Tree road.

For the first time the boy knew a pang of real jealousy. How could he hope to compete with a man like that. This chap had everything in the world to offer her; and he, nothing. And Etta deserved the best that there was. This chap could take her abroad, show her all the gay and wonderful things of life. Her own life would be immeasurably enriched by sheer proximity with his.

They were riding along slowly, laughing and chatting together, and once she reached out a hand and held on to his shoulder, allowing herself to be towed along by him as it were, with a gesture of such wonderful intimacy.

That night he went home and thought about nothing else.

And the very next evening he went to see her as usual.

He rode up just as she was on the point of saying goodnight to the same man, at the gate.

She seemed specially gay, and with a sparkle and brilliance that she lacked when she was alone with him.

'Joe, this is Mr Hurd,' she said. Just like that. Joe this is Mr Hurd; as though they knew all about each other.

The two men shook hands. And it seemed to Joe that they talked without that spontaneous gaiety between them now, as though his presence had caused something that glowed between them to be put out.

Presently the man shook hands again and rode off. And the boy and girl were left alone at the gate, facing each other. There was something a little defiant about her, he thought. But there was also, as it were, the last flicker of this new brilliance and sparkle, as though it still burned there within her mysteriously, albeit just a remnant now, giving off just a little glow, but enough to make her seem imperious, aloof.

'Coming in?' she said.

He followed her in through the gate without answering.

They went and sat in their usual place on the verandah.

She started off by being gay and debonair. But he wasn't having any of it.

'Who is he?' he said, coming directly to the point.

'Eh? Oh, you mean Mr Hurd. Why, Joe! whatever are you glooming like that about.' She burst out laughing.

'Look,' she said. 'Don't let us be silly. Mr Hurd is just a friend, that's all. Just a friend, see? If you want to know, he is married to the most wonderful wife, and they have the two dearest little kids, a boy and a girl. And he just adores them.'

Her words, the very way she spoke about it all, with that utter frankness, had the effect of instantly releasing that fierce tension inside him. But he didn't let it show right away. It was perhaps just as well for her to know that he could be jealous, that he wasn't going to stand for anything that wasn't as it ought to be, seeing how it was between them.

But after a while, and under her gentle teasing, he relented.

He went home that night feeling more than ever convinced that

Etta and he must get married soon. He would have to find a way to break down her resistance. Now that he was once and for all determined about it he knew that it could be done.

But the following night he found her in another mood again. There was something subdued, and dreamy and remote about her. Not bright and gay like she had been the night before, but as though something hushed and wonderful was happening inside her, even now; something that was not to be talked about, but hallowed, in the meaning of a treasured secret.

When he tried to talk about their getting married she wouldn't have any of it.

'Listen, Joe,' she said, patiently, taking him lightly by the sleeve. 'I have already told you that it is impossible. Let's just go on being friends, can't we? Perhaps later . . . I might change my mind . . . but not now. Not tonight, please.'

He left her that night feeling vaguely disturbed. But he couldn't tell what it was exactly that made him feel that way.

Weeks passed in a sort of hazy uncertainty, in which was inextricably mingled a kind of bitterness that was directed not against her but against those indefinable circumstances that are generally and loosely known as fate.

His life lay here, with her. His fate had become inextricably involved with hers. There was no way around it. And it irked him, feeling as he did that he could not have his life, all of it, all that it meant, until he had her.

He felt utterly wretched and utterly weary. He wanted to shut out everything, and for them to give up and yield utterly at last to each other, to find themselves within each other.

He found her one night even more wretched than he was, and ready to weep her eyes out on his shoulder.

'There. There,' he said, stroking her arm, dully. 'Don't be miserable, don't cry. It is all right. It will be all right. It must be all right.'

His own mute wretchedness now seemed a very far way off. It lay like something dead within him that he could not put away.

He stroked her hair, lightly; and when she put her head down on his shoulder, he placed both arms around her and drew her to him. But it seemed to him that he neither gave or took any comfort from this. Inside him, about him, everything seemed a waste of bitterness and barrenness, not to be put away, not to be shut out: and joy a thing forever lost, never to be restored. He felt suddenly betrayed and lost and wretched, without hope anywhere.

'Joe,' she whispered, 'Joe,' clinging to him with all her might, as though she wanted to reassure herself of the reality of him here, with her arms about him.

'It's all right, old girl. It's all right, I tell you. There.'

'Joe,' she said. 'It's happened. Oh God!'

'Happened?'

'I wasn't sure until yesterday.'

He held her a little away from him and tried to look into her eyes, as yet not sure of what she meant, not sure of himself, anything.

'You mean?'

'Yes, Joe.' She swallowed hard, looking at him with drooping mouth, and eyes that were swimming with tears. Her face seemed to him all drowned in tears, that was it. Just that.

He just sat there looking back at her, not knowing what to say; not sure of his own reactions, anything.

And suddenly she buried her head against his chest and started sobbing again.

'Joe,' she sobbed. 'Joe.'

'It's all right, I tell you,' he said, almost roughly.

'Oh, Joe, why do you look at me like that.'

'I was thinking, that's all. Can't you understand that'd make a fellow think? We've got to get married now, that's all.'

But somehow the realization of his life's happiness, coming so suddenly and unexpectedly this way, brought no upsurging revelation of joy with it. Not as he would have expected it to. Perhaps it was because it had all happened so suddenly. He hadn't had time to prepare for it. That was it. That was all.

'Joe.'

'Yes, dear.'

'Are you sure you still love me, Joe?'

'Of course I love you. Is that what's worrying you?'

'Say it, then. Say that you love me. I want to hear you say it.
Now, Joe.'

'I love you, Etta. You know I love you. How could you ever doubt
it.'

'And you will always love me, Joe, no matter what happens? For
ever and ever?'

'For ever and ever,' he said, with anguish in his voice.

Just a Little Love, a Little Kiss

SHE had quite a nice voice and was fond of singing. When the schoolmaster came to live in the house next door that had been empty for three months she was happy about it in a quiet way. The schoolmaster was a bachelor and his sister kept house for him.

Every afternoon she sang to them. She pretended it was to herself she was singing, of course, but in a half-conscious way she drew upon her unseen audience for inspiration and encouragement. Not that they ever spoke about it; and once or twice someone would turn on the radio next door just when she really got started. When that happened she would quietly leave the piano and take up her knitting. She would sit on the verandah and knit and watch Rover snoring on the mat or scratching behind his ear or searching his belly for fleas.

Once or twice she tried to ignore the radio and keep right on singing like it didn't matter, but her heart wasn't in it. And once when she wanted to phone the Corporation about the tap over the sink in the pantry needing a washer, she went across and asked if she might use their phone. She stopped to chat for a minute and then presently looked at her wrist-watch.

'My, it's almost time for tea,' she said. 'How quickly time flies.'

But they didn't ask her to stay for tea. Only smiled politely at her observation about the flight of time, and the sister walked with her as far as the front door.

The schoolmaster was a rather silent man with a hard uncompromising mouth, but she liked him. She wondered about him; why it was he had never married, and did he like living a bachelor's life, with his sister to keep house for him.

She sang in her rather sweet plaintive voice:

'*Just a little love, a little kiss* . . .', and 'Tropical Moon', thinking about the life of a schoolmaster, and how lonely it must be with nothing but succession after succession of incoming boys to brighten it, and each very much the same as the last.

'*Just a little love, a little kiss* . . .' she sang, while Rover sat on the carpet and chased fleas with restless energy and snapping teeth all the way from his belly to his rump.

After that first afternoon she got into the habit of going across to use the phone for one thing or another almost every afternoon.

She walked with the sister though the garden and said how pretty the flowers were, and asked the name of a yellow rose that grew by her little gate that divided the front garden from the backyard.

Then they walked through the back of the premises and she saw the duck that had come out recently with eleven dills. She picked upn one of the yellow dills and pressed it to her cheek.

'I love them. Don't you?'

They looked into each other's eyes and laughed, outwardly with the simplicity of children, but each secretly taking the measure of the other, in the way of women with women.

Her old father who stopped with relatives in the country and was ailing and lonely came up to live with her. She was happy to have the old man. He was fussy and irritable, but his presence gave her something to think about all day when she wasn't reading or playing the piano or singing to herself. It helped having him there, if only to take her mind off herself for a time, and to fill the empty spaces in her routine of living.

From her bedroom window she could see into the study next door. For the last three nights he had been up late, poring over examination papers he had taken home for correction. It was near the end of the Summer term when as a result of the examination certain boys would be moved up to higher forms, and it involved a lot of work.

She sat by her window long in the darkness watching him, knowing he could not see her.

She would undress in the dark, letting the clothes fall to the floor and stepping out of them daintily. Then she would go across to the window and raise her arms above her head, breathing deeply.

Then she would drop them to her sides, and fling them out before her, leaning back slightly, with something inside her straining, straining as though seeking to escape from her body altogether. Practising deep breathing before the open window.

Meanwhile over in his study he would be brooding over stacks of exercise books. She felt a great pitying yearning for him.

She would wrap herself in a gay little kimono and sit by the window, still, still as a little secret, until he put out his light, or until the sheer physical numbness brought about by her cramped position induced her to go to bed.

Once she played with the idea of putting on the light and standing naked and revealed, bathed in the mellow mazda-glow, while she did her exercises before the window. The study was dark for he had not yet come in. But no, she couldn't do it. What would he think of her if he should come in suddenly and see her! No, it was too bold. She could never bring herself to do that.

One night he was working even later than usual. Suddenly he sprang up from the desk like a man haunted and came and stood by the window, staring out. His dark figure in silhouette looked vague and brooding. He leaned against the window jamb and just stood looking out, the glow of the match flame from which he lit his pipe momentarily illuminated his face, and at intervals like that as it was sucked down into the bowl of the pipe, and alternately flared up again. It heightened the effect of melancholy brooding and unreality.

She drew back from the window involuntarily, with a little catch in her breath, her hands going to her breasts. But presently she smiled, knowing that if she did not move he could not see her.

She stood there for a long time scarcely breathing, not daring to move or make a sound against the palpable stillness of the garden that was all between them. Still, still as a little secret. And he stood there on his side of the fence, a man made restless and haunted with unconscious emotions that moved him with unfulfilled longings, and all the restless years of vagrant desires and idle dreams.

And then she conceived her great idea. Her splendid idea. She would play for him, sing to him. Sing as she had never sung before.

Tonight, now. She would lay all her heart bare in the witness of song. But song that would flow out from her in a pure and wonderful stream.

What did it matter that it was past midnight. That Dad who always slept lightly would be awakened. What did it matter about the neighbours . . . let *them* think what they may. Nothing must stop her. Now she must lay bare all her heart to him, in the pure and splended witness of song welling up from within her.

Quickly she slipped into her kimono and went out into the sitting room. Then breathlessly she started to play.

'*Just a little love, a little kiss* . . .' she sang. And 'Tropical Moon'.

But it wasn't so much the words, or the music, as herself revealed in them. Herself flowing out toward him in the wonder and beauty of longing and fulfilment; in all the mystery and meaning of a dream.

The next day she went about the house quiet as a mouse. A woman with a secret. Dad's nagging did not disturb her. Nothing could disturb that centre of stillness, of pure resolve, that she had found deep within her.

She didn't go next door that afternoon, either. Nor did she wonder about it much, finding one of the yellow dills dead on the lawn. She felt sorry for it. That it should be so innocent and dead, lying there on the lawn; but in a detached way, as she was about everything today. Without any comment upon it except its frailty and loveliness and innocence made all the more poignant by the stillness of death; and negative, without the meaning of life. About that, and nothing more.

And his sister at the fence saying something . . . She looked up as though starting out of a dream; her hand at her throat, looking up with bright eyes to meet the sister's dark resentful ones.

Poor Edward, he was having a trying time, the sister said. He was working too hard, that's what. A good thing the holidays were almost here. They were going away to the hills for the Summer. Some place where it would be quiet and cool.

People didn't know the meaning of quiet, she said.

And she almost wanted to hug her for saying that. It was precisely what she had been thinking herself all morning. The meaning of quiet . . . The pure mysticism and ecstasy of that inner quiet, the *innerness* of it giving it meaning.

He slept very badly last night, the sister said, her watery eyes looking away. And he couldn't work. If she didn't look out he would be getting a nervous breakdown. He couldn't rest for the noise last night. Once she heard him moving about the house. Then she heard him at the back door. When she went outside she found him in the backyard with the shot gun. He had though he had heard a thief prowling around in the chicken run.

That night she went to bed early with a splitting headache.

She was awake when the shot gun went off. The sound of it made her jump violently. Her nerves. She went across to the window quickly and threw it open from the bottom. She was on the point of calling out, only everything was so terrifyingly still she was afraid to make a sound. She crept quietly back to bed.

The next morning she found to her dismay that Rover had been shot in the side, but he wasn't dead, though he was breathing his last, lying on the mat outside the door. She remembered the shot she had heard in the night. The dead dill on the lawn. Things came back to her with a rush.

How could he! How *could* he! She thought of the cold uncompromising set of his mouth, a little cruel, and her eyes filled with tears.

She went and phoned for the vet, but she didn't use their phone.

Rover was still alive when the vet came but nothing could be done for him. He was almost gone. Yes, he must have suffered a great deal. Too bad.

People didn't know the meaning of quiet . . . His sister's voice speaking. It all came back to her now. The dead dill on the lawn. *He slept very badly last night* . . . *Couldn't rest for the noise* . . . She had been playing the piano, singing . . . *'Just a little love, a little kiss . . .'* 'Tropical Moon'. It all came back to her now with a rush that brought the tears to her eyes. She put her head down in her hands and wept bitterly. She felt of a sudden the bleakness and loneliness of her thirty-seven years overtaking her.

She went and made herself a cup of tea, and bathed her eyes.

Then she went next door – not to their house, to the house across the street – and telephoned the police. Later a policeman arrived on a bicycle and took a statement.

Then he went off to the station and made out the summons. Cruelty to animals. Shooting a dog.

She felt old and ugly in the witness box, and all dried up inside. He was given the option of paying a fine of twenty shillings, or going to prison for thirty days. He paid the fine. It came out in court that the shotgun wasn't licensed, or that he wasn't licensed to use a shotgun, she forgot which. For that he was reprimanded by the magistrate.

She passed him on the steps outside the courthouse. He lifted his hat gravely, but she only saw it out of the corner of her eye, for she wasn't looking at him.

The following week the brother and sister went away to the hills – to some place where it was cool and quiet, to spent their holidays.

And worst of all she hasn't even the comfort of her music any longer. Because, for some reason or another, she won't even go near the piano any more.

The Month of the Beautiful Stranger

THE boy of course had known nothing about love. He was too young. And he had been brought up all his life in the country. What time he had not spent on his father's property he had been at boarding school. A particularly cloistered one this, intended principally for the sons of parsons. No doubt the idea being to bring up these boys the way parsons' sons ought to be brought up.

And then one Midsummer holiday he learnt to his dismay that his mother was having a stranger in the house for a whole month. A young woman. In addition to his natural shyness of strangers he disliked girls intensely. And the reason for this dislike arose out of a very natural and perhaps ordinary occurrence. It had happened when he was a little boy of seven or so. At that time his parents had lived in the city and he was sent to one of those private preparatory-kindergarten schools.

One day he was behind the shelter of a clump of palm trees in the garden performing that perfectly normal function of nature, and the simple conventions that govern the style in which a small boy's trousers should be cut, enables him to accomplish with the maximum of ease, and even with a certain unselfconscious dignity. But in the midst of this operation he was discovered by a troop of hoydenish girls somewhat older than himself. The ringleader was one particular vixen with red hair, who, irrespective of sex, was quite the most inveterate tease in all the school.

To affront the dignity of a boy of seven is something quite unforgivable. He had been laughed at, and generally made the sport of these unspeakably vulgar little girls, and his sense of outrage was such that for many years he was unable to forget it. Indeed the memory of that incident remained as clear in his mind now as hough it had happened yesterday.

The fact that the young lady was quite the most beautiful person he had ever seen only made the boy resent her presence the more. He was downright rude to her whenever the occasion offered. He resolutely snubbed all her tentative advances of friendliness. But she seemed not to notice all this, not to mind it at all, and his parents wisely refrained from making any special comment on his behaviour toward their guest.

But one day when he was out in the common with his sling-shot taking a pot at some ground doves that had their feeding ground in a wooded hollow where there was a spring, he suddenly came upon her sitting under a tree. She was reading a book. The book lay open on her knees. She was in the act of licking her finger preparatory to turning the page when he became aware of her presence. The whole unconscious poise of her, that little gesture, everything, clearly indicated that she was entirely unaware of being observed.

He stood for a long time without moving. Just watching her. The unselfconscious grace of her, the delicately curved and infinitely gracious lines of her in profile, all the way down to her little feet that were drawn up so that she appeared almost to be sitting on them. He remained standing there for about five minutes, afraid to move or make a sound. Almost holding his breath in the urgency of not making her aware of his presence. And then he withdrew as silently as a shadow beyond the screen of bushes and trees.

When he was out of sight and earshot he started running very swiftly across the common and he didn't stop until he stood panting on the other side of the barbed wire fence that entirely enclosed it.

He looked about him almost guiltily to see if anyone was about who might have observed his actions, and having satisfied himself he thrust his hands in his pockets and sauntered carelessly up the path that led to the house, whistling loudly and untunefully as he went. The sling-shot dangled half out of his pocket giving the suggestion of a dispirited tail.

At tea that afternoon he was even ruder than usual. He took great pains to show her that anything like conversation with her was distinctly distasteful to him. He reached right across her helping

himself to things rather than ask her to pass them, and merel[y]
nodded his head, once when she addressed him directly. She eve[n]
made a hole in a slice of bread and looked at him with one grea[t]
eye through this, but he wasn't amused.

For her part she didn't seem to mind greatly. And once she mad[e]
his ears burn, kicking off her shoes and climbing up a tree as though
she had been doing that sort of thing all her life. His eyes fascinated,
followed her as she went up and up, and she didn't seem to mind
a bit; not the fact that all that much pink flesh should show, nor
yet his obvious embarrassment at seeing it.

'You're only trying to show off,' he said, standing at the foot
of the tree and gazing up at her, his eyes screwed up against the
light.

She made a face at him and laughed. A bright note like a bird's
that went tinkling across the silence, and out and away.

He flushed to the roots of his hair, burning all the while with
unspeakable anger.

'I suppose you think that's very funny,' he said, lamely. He
wanted to say something cutting. Something that would slay the
laughing sprite in her, outright. But all he could manage was that
rather lame: 'I suppose you think that's very funny.'

And the thought of the inadequacy of his weapons against her
only sharpened his anger. So that in order to save the shreds of
his dignity he had to thrust his hands in his pockets and saunter
carelessly down the path, whistling with sudden tremendous zest.

Two weeks passed and still the boy gave no sign of changing his
attitude toward her. But you could see that while she took it almost
as a matter of course, the strain of keeping it up was telling on him,
making him more and more sullen and unhappy looking.

And then his mother decided it was time someone should take
notice of it. She did this in what she considered a tactful manner.
She started teasing him mildly when they were alone about his being
in love with the young woman.

'I believe you are, too,' she insisted, looking up at him from
plucking at a loose thread on the tablecloth, when he offered no
reply.

He got up abruptly and walked away.

She called him by his name. 'Come here,' she said, in a tone of quiet authority.

But he sulked and refused to sit down again.

'Silly,' she said. Just that. But her tone implied more. It told him that she and everyone else thought he was making a fool of himself. But by now he was in a thoroughly rebellious mood, and he didn't care what anyone might choose to think.

'I believe you're afraid. A little boy afraid to grow up. That's all,' she said.

So she believed he was afraid. Now what did she mean by that? Well, just to show them that he jolly well *wasn't* afraid of anyone he went and deliberately sought her out.

She was reading a book under a tree in the garden. The same book. He recognised it by the green cover. He came and stood before her with an almost challenging gesture, his hands thrust deep in his pockets, leaning backward slightly from the waist, and alternately raising and lowering himself on his toes. The way he thought it was proper for a man to stand when he wanted to impress people that he wasn't scared of nothing or no one.

'What's that book you're reading?' he said, without preamble, as he might have been a cop questioning a character suspected of being in unlawful possession of something.

'Why, it's just a book I picked up in the house somewhere,' she said.

Was he frowning at her? She didn't know what to make of it.

'Is it yours?' she asked, with a disarming smile.

'I don't read that kind of book. Love stories and all that trash. That's for girls and sissies.'

'Oh!' she said.

'Look here,' he said, 'what you want to read all that stuff for.'

'It's a very interesting story.'

'Girls are all the same,' he said, standing on his toes and looking down at her from that superior elevation.

'My, what a man of the world you must be.'

'Me? Why yes. I've been around.'

'Of course,' she said, properly impressed.

She was several years older than he, and in her own quiet way

157

had seen a considerable slice of life herself.

'Don't let all that stuff go to your head, all you do,' he said oracularly, as he sauntered off with what he considered the utmost carelessness.

When he threw a surreptitious glance over his shoulder at her, she wasn't even smiling.

But somehow he didn't feel greatly comforted as a result of this encounter. He realized deep down that it was all a bravado, that he had accomplished nothing, proved nothing.

And then the following week she went away. And he knew he would never see her again.

Somehow the dreadful certainty of it was like a deadening blow. And it was only then, after she had gone, and out of his life forever, that he realized that he loved her as he would never love another. And she would forget him in a little while, he knew. Quite forget that he even existed.

All the pain and the loneliness of the ensuing days was too much even to try to tell of it. For the poignant suffering of youth is something quite different again. Something we can only vaguely remember, looking back upon it in retrospect. But never again experience, as adults. Not with the same keen edge of the knowledge of anguish beyond hope; with all our knowledgeableness, with all our larger experience, ever.

He grew thinner and more silent as the days went by. He knew, once and for all, that he would never be able to forget her. Not if he lived to be a hundred. And at the same time there seemed nothing in life left for him to live for.

In the night it was worse. He would sit up in his bed with the cover drawn above his knees and stare out into the darkness and see only her face. Every movement and fleeting expression of it. Every incomparable, least, transitory shade of expression, of light and laughter, of mingled mischievousness and loveliness not to be told again.

He would sit there, hugging his knees to him, and go through all the agony of remembering, shivering every once in a while with the cold wind that came down from the mountains – until late into the night. His soul plumbed the last unutterable depth of loneliness, of emptiness and despair. Until he was wrung out of all feeling, beyond the last possible reach of anguish that the human mind may know. Until he became like a stone, without feeling, without thought. Without sense of time or motion.

He knew what it was truly to be dead, without life or the knowledge of existence past. Dead like the cold heart lying beneath a great immovable stone. He tasted death, and knew the otherness of that state. And all the process and agony that separates the two. Until utterly exhausted he fell asleep.

And then one day his mother received a letter from the girl. It was just a simple, conventional little note, but he watched her face with all the agony of expectancy that tries deliberately to efface itself behind a mask of indifference. Because he couldn't bear the thought that she might discover his secret and tease him about it. It would be a desecration of his fine sorrow, that was something apart, to endure himself alone, in the secret places of his heart.

But he must see what she had written in the letter. Perhaps she had not forgotten him quite. Perhaps if he were able to read between the lines there would be something for him to hope upon. Or forever utterly to damn all hope.

Without the slightest compunction therefore he possessed himself of the letter, and taking it privily to his room, read it behind the locked door.

He read it through twice, three times. And after that he sat for a time just staring at the pages, without seeing the writing that covered them.

She had said nothing about him. It was a simple, straightforward letter, as any girl might write in similar circumstances. There was absolutely nothing to be read between the lines.

Quietly he folded the pages and returned them to the envelope, then he sneaked it back into his mother's room where she had left it.

That afternoon although the ground doves called from their feeding place in the hollow down by the common he avoided the spot. Skirting all the way around it he went in search of other feeding places further afield. And came home in the evening tired, showing many scratches and bruises and empty-handed.

Strangely enough his mother laughed quite happily when she saw him coming in with the dusk.

'My, I thought you were lost,' she said, flippantly.

He just stood and looked at her, deep reproach in his sombre eyes. And then he went in to his supper. He ate in silence thinking about his mother and deep down in his heart forgiving her for her flippancy. He thought a little bitterly of the vaunted intuition of women. For how could Mother understand, he mused, chewing thoughtfully on a large mouthful of lemon pie. In the wonderful and mysterious way of mothers she thought of him still as a boy. How *could* she know, having no access to that special knowledge, that already he had grown to the full stature of a man.